THE ABRAHAM ENIGMA

THE ABRAHAM ENIGMA

JACK LYON

DESERET
BOOK

Salt Lake City, Utah

Images on pages 3, 53, and 111 from Shutterstock.

Image of "Caractors" transcript on page 95, from Ariel L. Crowley, "The Anthon Transcript," in *Improvement Era,* February 1942, 77.

Images on pages 151, 152, 153, 157, and 160 from Wikimedia Commons. All other images in public domain.

Visit us at DeseretBook.com

Library of Congress Cataloging-in-Publication Data

Lyon, Jack M.
    The Abraham enigma / Jack Lyon.
        p.   cm.
    Sequel to: The Moroni code.
    Includes bibliographical references.
    Summary: When FBI agent and cryptologist David Hunter is temporarily assigned to decipher coded terrorist communications in Egypt, he turns to an unlikely source for help—an authentic Egyptian document containing the pharaohs' priestly writing code, hieroglyphics that bear a remarkable similarity to characters in the fascimiles in the Book of Abraham.
    ISBN 978-1-60641-106-3 (paperbound)
    1. Mormons—Fiction.   2. Terrorists—Fiction.   3. Book of Abraham—Fiction.
    4. Suspense fiction.   I. Title.
    PS3612.Y559A24 2010
    813'.6—dc22   2010019686

Printed in the United States of America
Malloy Lithographing Incorporated, Ann Arbor, MI

10   9   8   7   6   5   4   3   2   1

For Colin Douglas,

teacher and friend

Ozymandias

I met a traveller from an antique land
　　Who said: "Two vast and trunkless legs of stone
Stand in the desert. Near them, on the sand,
　　Half sunk, a shattered visage lies, whose frown,
And wrinkled lip, and sneer of cold command
　　Tell that its sculptor well those passions read
Which yet survive (stamped on these lifeless things)
　　The hand that mocked them, and the heart that fed.
And on the pedestal these words appear—
　　'My name is Ozymandias, king of kings:
Look on my works, ye Mighty, and despair!'
　　Nothing beside remains. Round the decay
Of that colossal wreck, boundless and bare
　　The lone and level sands stretch far away."

—Percy Bysshe Shelley

Introductory Note

Although this book can be read on its own, it is also a sequel to my previous book, *The Moroni Code*. If you haven't read it, here's a bit of background that will help you understand what's going on:

- David Hunter is an FBI agent stationed in Salt Lake City. His specialty is cryptography—the deciphering of secret code.
- April McKenzie is a researcher who works at the Church History Library. She helped David in his quest to decipher Joseph Smith's transcription of characters from the gold plates.

And of course, they fell in love . . .

PROLOGUE

Abasi Mubarak thought about smoking one last cigarette before blowing himself up. But really, what was the point? He'd already been circling the streets of Cairo for more than an hour, periodically cruising past the American ambassador's residence, trying to work up the courage to crash through the security gate and drive his cargo of bombs headlong into the brown limestone mansion, blowing an entire wing of the building to smithereens. At least that was the plan. The council had provided handsomely for Abasi's aging parents, who would be losing their son but gaining a hero—and the prestige that went with it. But if he didn't follow through soon, he knew he would back out, bringing derision upon himself and shame upon his family.

This time around, he thought, dismayed by his own hesitation, *if the guard has looked away, I will do it.*

Again he drove past the mansion, peering into the window of the guardhouse. To his surprise, it was empty. But no—the back of the guard's head appeared at the bottom of the window. He'd bent down to pick something up—something he'd dropped, perhaps—providing a momentary distraction. The time had come.

Abasi slowed the car, turned into the driveway that led past the guardhouse, and then stomped on the accelerator. The guard looked up, startled, but it was too late—the car was already crashing through the wooden gate, the broken boards flying up against the windshield, the guard shouting at him to stop. Abasi heard the sound of gunfire and felt a sudden burning in his shoulder, but the pain only fueled his anger, his determination.

Then, suddenly, the whole world went silent. And, he realized, it wasn't the car that was moving. It was everything *else* that was moving. From the heart of stillness he watched, entranced, as trees sped past, as an unwary visitor thumped into the car's grill, as the building rushed forward to meet him, its walls looming ever larger, its windows growing ever darker.

And then, strangely, he became one with the building. Its walls were his body, its windows his eyes. He heard an explosion; then the sound blew out his eardrums. He saw his hands burning; then his eyes burst from their sockets. He breathed black smoke and rock dust; then his lungs collapsed. After that, he knew no more.

PART 1

CHAPTER 1

The newly married April Hunter stepped shyly out of the elegant bathroom at the Grand America Hotel in Salt Lake City. Her blonde hair was down, curling about her shoulders, and her white satin nightgown seemed to glow in the muted light of the spacious honeymoon suite. Leaning against the door frame, she smiled at David, who was already in bed.

"Well?" she said. "What do you think?"

"Uh . . . ," he managed to get out. "I . . . um . . . uh . . ."

"That bad, huh?" She tilted her head.

"No! I just . . ." He coughed. "I seem to have stopped breathing."

"You probably need a little CPR." She walked slowly to the bed, then bent down and kissed him softly. When he started to kiss her back, she blew forcefully into his lungs.

David sat up, gasping. "Hey!"

April laughed. "What's the matter? I thought you needed help."

"You're the one who's going to need help!" David pulled her onto the bed. "The problem is, you didn't do it right. Here, let me show you."

April screamed, then pretended to struggle as he held her down, kissing her over and over, until she finally stopped resisting.

April lay cozily against David's chest, his arm curled around her shoulders. "Well," she said, "it's been quite a day."

"It sure has."

"What was your favorite part?"

"Looking at you over the altar."

April sighed. "Yes, that must have been nice for you." Her eyes twinkled.

David started to laugh. "You really are something, you know that?"

"I do try."

He kissed the top of her head. "What was *your* favorite part?"

April thought for a moment. "I loved all of it—just all of it. I loved going through the temple. We should keep going back—a lot. We can even get married for other people—do sealings, I mean. And we can do endowments."

"Sure," David said. "That would be good."

"You don't sound so sure."

"Oh, I'm fine." He shook his head. "There's just so much I didn't understand."

"Well, it *is* a unique experience."

"I'll say."

"But it was good, right?"

"Yes, very good." David paused. "It felt good to be there. And the symbolism is fascinating. Maybe I just need to go through a session a few more times."

April smiled. "It might take more than a few."

"Well, that's encouraging. Did you understand it?"

"Parts of it."

"Yeah, me too."

April rolled onto her back. "They say you learn more as you keep going back."

"That's what my grandma said."

"And you *like* to learn."

David smiled. "That's true—I do. Maybe we should go back tomorrow."

April sat up. "Really? Tomorrow?"

"Why not? We're on our honeymoon; we can do whatever we want."

"Mmm. I love it. Let's never go back to work."

"Work? What's that?"

༄

As it turned out, they did go to the temple the next day—after a late and leisurely breakfast at the hotel. As they walked, the morning air sparkled with sunshine, and the tulips and daffodils near the temple entrance provided brilliant splashes of reds and yellows against the gray granite walls. Much to his surprise, David found himself thinking about the contrast—the recurring growth, then death, of the fragile flowers compared to the enduring strength of the stone building. Was the temple itself a symbol of eternity?

David turned to April. "I think I just learned something new," he said in a low voice.

She squeezed his hand. "No fair! We're not even inside yet."

"Maybe that's how it works."

"So what did you learn?" April looked at him inquisitively.

"The temple is a symbol of eternity."

Feigning shock, April replied, "You didn't know that?"

David grinned. "I'm doing the best I can here, okay?"

They passed through the temple's gleaming doorway and approached the large, white-haired man at the recommend desk—"Brother Robbins," his name badge said. He checked their recommends, then looked at David and April over the top of his glasses. "Weren't you here yesterday? Just married?"

David nodded.

The man smiled broadly. "And you're coming back already? Good for you! Welcome to the House of the Lord."

During the session, David did understand more—or at least saw things he hadn't noticed before. Thinking about the symbols as he would a code, he saw that they had a sequence, and that there was meaning not only in the symbols but also in their various parts—the symbols that made up the symbols, so to speak. But he had the feeling that some larger picture was eluding him, that the meaning of the experience was much deeper than the symbols themselves.

Look higher, the Spirit seemed to whisper. *Open your mind to a greater knowledge.* But that, he realized, might take a while; he'd need to keep coming back. So for now, he tried to relax and enjoy the presentation, which wasn't hard to do. The elderly people taking part seemed so sweet and sincere, and one of the actors said his lines in such a droll way that everyone in the session chuckled from time to time.

After the session, David stopped for a minute to speak to Brother Robbins at the recommend desk. The man was busy with a patron coming into the temple, but after checking her recommend he turned to David.

"Did you enjoy your session?"

"Yes, thanks." David said. "But could I ask you a quick question?"

"Certainly."

"I'd like to learn more about the temple. What books of scripture would best help with that?"

Brother Robbins thought for a moment. "Well, the book of Moses, in the Pearl of Great Price, covers some of the same material as the endowment. You'll see a lot of parallels."

"Okay," David said.

"But personally . . . I'd go with the book of Abraham." The big man nodded.

"I've never thought of that as being related to the temple."

"But when you read it in the past, you hadn't been to the temple, had you."

David shook his head.

"Give it another try; you might be surprised at what you find."

"Okay. I will. Thanks a lot."

"You're welcome." Brother Robbins smoothed back his white hair. "Now, if you'll excuse me, I need to get back to work." He nodded to the new group of patrons who were coming through the door. Then he leaned over and whispered, "I wouldn't want them to dock my paycheck." He winked at David.

David took April by the hand. "Let's get back to the hotel. I have some reading to do."

She reached up and patted his cheek. "Sorry, but we have other plans."

The next day, Friday, April wanted to eat lunch at a sushi restaurant on 200 West—something David wasn't so sure about. As they walked inside, the place was packed with customers crowding around the tiny tables. Some diners sat on stools at the sushi bar, watching the chefs' elegant chopping.

"Raw fish," David said with a shudder. "Are you sure about this?"

"For an FBI agent, you're not very brave."

"Okay, okay. But let's not get anything too weird."

"Of course not." April smiled. "We'll start with my favorite—octopus."

David blanched. "I'm not eating anything with tentacles."

"Just kidding. We'll get you a California roll. You'll love the fake crab!"

David grimaced. "That doesn't sound so good either."

April rolled her eyes.

After a five-minute wait, the waiter escorted them to a tiny black table. April ordered for both of them but held on to the colorful menu so she could show David the different kinds of sushi. Just as she was getting started, David's cell phone rang. Surprised, he pulled it out of his pocket, then looked at the screen.

"It's my boss," he said, opening the phone and putting it to his ear.

"Hello, Hunter." The familiar voice boomed into the tiny earpiece, and in his mind's eye, David saw his fifty-something director—his graying hair, his deep-set eyes—whose expert marksmanship had saved David's life on more than one occasion.

"Agent Wilcox! What's going on?"

"Sorry to bother you on your honeymoon."

"That's okay. We're just getting ready to have lunch. Is something wrong?"

"No, nothing's wrong. But I have a proposal you might be interested in."

"What kind of proposal?" David winked at April, who was frowning and drumming her fingers on the table.

"Remember our talk about that promotion you want—the job at Washington, D.C.?"

"Sure." David sat up a little straighter.

"Well, I'm taking that seriously. So when you return to the office next week, I'll have a new assignment for you—the U.S. embassy in Cairo, Egypt. We'll see how you do, and then figure out what happens next."

"Wow, Egypt! No kidding?"

April stopped drumming her fingers.

"That's right. But here's the catch: I was thinking you might want to take April and go early—as part of your honeymoon. We'll be flying you there anyway, but your buddies here at the office have taken up a collection so April can go along. And she can stay till the end of your assignment. What do you think?"

David was stunned. "That's . . . that's just so nice of everybody. I really didn't expect anything like this."

"I hear the pyramids look pretty amazing in the moonlight."

"I'll bet they do." He glanced over at April. "I'd like to talk to April about this. Can I call you back?"

"Of course."

But April was shaking David's shoulder.

"Hold on a second." David covered the mouthpiece, trying to look nonchalant. "What is it, April dear?"

"What about Egypt? What's going on?"

"Agent Wilcox wants to send me on assignment—*after* our honeymoon."

April breathed a sigh of relief.

"But he's offered to send both of us early as *part* of our honeymoon. What do you think?"

"Are you kidding?" April bounced up and down in her seat. "That would be great!"

David went back to the phone, laughing. "I guess we don't need to talk about it. April is ready to go."

"Good. You'll be staying with an old friend of mine—I'll fill you in on the details later. You can leave whenever you're ready, but I've already found a flight that looks pretty good. It leaves tomorrow at 8:30 A.M. You'll be in Cairo by 11:00 A.M.—Cairo time, of course—the following morning."

David looked over at April. "Want to leave tomorrow morning?"

"Tomorrow morning? No! We'll need time to get ready."

"Wilcox? How about the next day?"

"Just a sec." David could hear Wilcox tapping on his computer keyboard. "Here's the same flight a day later—departure time 8:30 A.M. That's Sunday, you realize."

"Hmmm. I'd rather not travel on Sunday if we can help it."

"Right. But even if you left tomorrow, you'd be getting into Cairo on Sunday—they're eight hours ahead of us. And next week you'll actually start work on Sunday—the day the embassy reopens after the Jewish Sabbath. Things are on a little different schedule there. By the way, with the time change, you'll basically get an extra day of honeymoon."

"Well, in that case . . ."

"Okay, then. You'll be leaving Sunday morning and getting into Cairo on Monday. Have your passports ready. We'll send a car to pick you up—say, 5:00 A.M. Your place?"

David groaned.

"Well, it is an international flight; you'll need plenty of time at the airport."

"Okay. We'll be ready."

"Oh, and one more thing. You should know that the FBI partner assigned to you in Cairo has also applied for the promotion in Washington."

David swallowed. "Well, that should make things interesting."

"I'm sure you'll be able to keep things on a professional level."

"Part of the job, right?"

"That's right."

"Okay, then. Thanks. I'll talk to you soon."

David closed the phone, then held both of April's hands over the table, looking into her eyes. In a crooning voice he said, "Wilcox says the pyramids are beautiful in the moonlight."

But April was holding back tears. "David, this is just so wonderful! I . . . I don't know what to say."

He laughed. "I knew life with you was going to be an adventure. I just didn't think it would start so soon."

CHAPTER 2

Runihura Badawi was growing impatient. The summer weather was gloriously hot in Cairo, and he'd had a fine lunch of couscous with shrimp at the Café of Mirrors just around the corner. Now he wanted an ice cream cone, which he planned to enjoy while strolling through the market. But an American woman in line ahead of him was letting her three children choose their own flavors, and the smallest boy was having a hard time deciding.

"Wouldn't you like chocolate?" the mother asked. "It's your favorite at home."

The boy looked up at her solemnly, his soulful brown eyes brimming with tears. "I want orange."

"I already told you, they don't have orange." The mother knelt down and took the boy's hands. "They have strawberry. Would you like strawberry?"

The boy shook his head.

But Runihura had had enough. "*I'd* like strawberry," he said loudly. "Everyone here would like *something*." He waved his skinny arms. "Just take your brats and get out of the way so the rest of us can order." He looked at the people behind him for support, but they were all staring at the pavement or looking with concern at the mother, who was now standing up to face her opponent.

"He's just a little boy," she said. "Surely you can be patient for a minute or two."

Runihura drew himself up stiffly. "I've been patient long enough. Either get something for the boy or get out of the way." He drew his fingers through his dark, greasy hair.

But the shopkeeper was signaling to one of the "tourist police" stationed nearby. The officer moved quickly across the plaza, then stood protectively in front of the woman, his hand ready on the pistol at his side. "Is there a problem here?"

Runihura shook his head. "We're just trying to order some ice cream."

An older man in line behind Runihura spoke up. "This man is causing trouble for the Americans."

The officer lifted his chin, his steady gaze fixed on Runihura. "Leave these people alone. Go buy your ice cream somewhere else." The officer frowned. "Such a big man, picking on women and children."

Runihura glared. "They're Americans. They have no business here."

"If you want a fight, I'll give you one. Don't make me warn you again."

Runihura lowered his eyes. He walked casually away across the plaza, but inside he was seething. If the Americans would just *get out,* stop interfering, the plan could go forward. *But it will not be long now,* he thought. *We will take care of the Americans—and their supporters— soon enough.* He would just have to learn to be patient.

❦

It was FBI agent Pam Lawford's first day at the U.S. embassy in Cairo, and already she could see that the work ahead of her was going to be much more complicated than she'd anticipated. Her assigned partner was on his way, but he was on his honeymoon—she rolled her eyes at the thought—and wouldn't be at the embassy for another week. That was all right; she could use the additional time to get ready for him.

The embassy building itself was huge, a blocky limestone monolith that towered over the surrounding area. The U.S. State Department had provided an office for Pam deep in the basement, but it was really not much more than a closet with two workstations, each with a desk, a chair, and a computer. She didn't mind so much; she'd been spending most of her time becoming familiar with embassy procedures and trying to figure out which workers might be most sympathetic to the terrorist cause. Some, she knew, were being less than stringent in providing visas for travelers to the United States. Here and there, terrorists were getting through—sometimes they were being *let* through.

Some of the embassy workers were obviously loyal to their jobs and to the United States; others were blatant in their dislike of Americans. Pam had made only a few friends so far. With her dark hair and olive skin, she fit in better than some of the other agents, but her command of Arabic was a bit rough, and her speech and mannerisms often gave her away. Most of the employees simply ignored her, but they all knew who she was and why she was there. And considering that this was an embassy of the United States of America, Pam was surprised at some of the posters the workers had taped to the walls of their cubicles—pictures with captions like "Islam: The New American Religion" and "Up with Hamas." Images of American mosques were posted everywhere.

Pam watched as a middle-aged man handed his visa application to one of the workers—a tall, angular woman named Nekhbet Rahman, according to the plastic sign in front of her window. Nekhbet looked through the application papers, then peered up at the man. "You are traveling to New Jersey?"

"Yes," the man said.

"What is the purpose of your visit?"

"I'm going to donate a kidney to my brother. See—I wrote it on the paper."

She shook her head. "I can't approve this application."

"Why not?" The man's voice was filled with dismay.

"What's that around your neck?"

"A gold chain." The man put his hand to his collar.

"You will show me, please."

"No. You have no right."

"It is a cross, is it not?"

"Yes!" the man hissed. "I am a Christian. I am not ashamed."

"You will take off that cross. Then perhaps I can approve your application."

The man raised his head defiantly. "I will not remove it."

"Very well." Nekhbet picked up a rubber stamp.

"Wait, wait," the man said. He rubbed his face, his distress clearly evident. Finally he took off the chain and cross, placing them in his pocket. "There," he said. "Now will you please approve my application?"

"No," Nekhbet said. She stamped the paper—REJECTED, in large red letters. "You are not trustworthy. You refused to show me your cross when I asked you. Your application has been denied."

"You don't care if I'm trustworthy or not," the man said. "You denied my application because I'm a Christian."

"That's ridiculous. We're not partial to one sect or another. I've already explained my decision, which is final."

The man shook his head, then raised his finger in warning. "You will hear more of this, I assure you." He turned and stalked out of the building.

Nekhbet turned to a coworker—Haqikah Wanly, according to

the sign at her window. "You see how quickly these Christians will renounce their faith. They are traitors, cowards. A Muslim would die first, would sacrifice his own life for Islam."

Haqikah nodded slightly but didn't look up. She just kept shuffling through her papers.

"Pfah," Nekhbet said. "You're as bad as they are." She recorded the transaction on the computer, then stood up. "Watch my window; I'm taking a break."

Pam watched as the woman stalked off. She found it interesting to see where people's allegiances lay—something she'd been thinking about a lot lately. And things were going to get even more complicated when her FBI partner got here—David Hunter from Salt Lake City. Of course, she had a job to do, she thought with a frown. But it wouldn't hurt if he turned out to be good-looking.

Haqikah looked around carefully to make sure no one was watching. Nekhbet was still on break—taking her time, as usual—and the American woman had gone back to her office. She stepped over to Nekhbet's computer and clicked back to the Christian man's profile. With a few keystrokes, she approved the man's application and added instructions to send the visa to his home address.

She closed the application, her hands hovering over the keyboard. She had a thought: It would be an easy matter to make other changes as well—to cancel approvals for people she knew to be terrorists. But not now—it wouldn't do to be caught by Nekhbet. She would have other opportunities.

CHAPTER 3

B y the time the newlyweds got to Egypt on Monday, April was no longer excited. In fact, she was starting to wish they'd stayed home. After the nearly five-hour flight to New York, they'd had a three-hour layover—not enough time to see anything— and the flight from New York to Cairo had taken eleven more hours. She'd found it hard to sleep on the plane—the seats being less than comfortable—and now, forty-five minutes after landing, the pilot wouldn't let the passengers leave the plane because of a security problem at the airport.

April's exasperation had finally turned into resignation, and then into fatigue. Feeling groggy, she rubbed her eyes. Back in Salt Lake City, it was the middle of the night, and all she really wanted to do was go to bed. But since that wasn't an option, she got up to go to the bathroom and wash her face. She was just stepping into the aisle when the pilot announced that the security problem had been cleared and the passengers could take their carry-on bags and disembark.

David groaned. "Finally!"

"Let's get out of here," April said.

They grabbed their bags from the overhead bin and stumbled their way down the aisle to the door, then through the accordion-like passage and out into the airport. To April's surprise, the airport was huge—ultra-modern and glistening with glass and steel. After a long walk through the terminal, they picked up their luggage—two big black suitcases sporting wheels and extendable handles.

Rolling the suitcases into the main lobby, they spotted a large, dark man who was holding up a white cardboard sign with lettering in black marker: "HUNTER." April noticed the man's curly black-and-gray hair and his carefully trimmed beard. Dressed all in white, he made an imposing figure.

"That must be our contact," David said.

April laughed. "And are spies watching us?"

"Maybe."

The thought sobered April. "Is it safe here?"

"From what I've read, yes. As long as you don't try to go somewhere you shouldn't—like a military base or a minefield. But places like that will be guarded or fenced."

As they approached the man with the sign, he extended a large, beefy hand. "Are you David Hunter?"

"Yes. And this is my wife, April."

"*As-salaamu-alaikum*—May peace be with you."

"*Wa al-alaikum as-salaam,*" David replied. "And with you."

"Very good," the man said. "You have studied Arabic?"

"Yes, as part of my antiterrorist training."

"You'll find it very useful here, although many people speak at least some English. And you, Mrs. Hunter?"

"Just English. And some French. But please, call me April."

"Very well. I am honored to be your host—Minkabh Hamid Elgabri. I would be happy if you would simply call me Minkabh."

"All right, Minkabh," David said. "Thanks for letting us stay with you."

"It is my pleasure. I have been a friend to the FBI for many years—my mother was an American. But let us go. My wife will have lunch ready. And I have a car waiting outside."

As they stepped through the automatic doors and out of the gleaming, air-conditioned lobby, the heat washed over April like a blast from a furnace, the sunlight glaring from a giant stainless-steel globe in front of the airport's tall glass windows. Down the road, as far as she could see, lines of palm trees sheltered the jumble of cars that were picking up or dropping off passengers. A man wearing a red turban wheeled past on a bicycle. And, in the distance, hundreds of minarets rose over the shining city—Cairo, "The Triumphant," waiting to be explored.

Minkabh's car wasn't just a car; it was a long, black Mercedes-Benz C300 luxury sedan with tinted windows and sparkling chrome wheels. The trunk was open, and a uniformed driver was standing in front of the open doors, smoking a cigarette.

"David, April, this is my driver, Donkor." As the driver lifted his cap, Minkabh started putting the luggage into the trunk.

"I can get those, sir," Donkor said.

"No, no. Please help Mr. and Mrs. Hunter into the car."

"Very well, sir."

April thought they didn't really need any help, but Donkor stood nearby, carefully closing the doors after they were settled into the soft leather seats.

Minkabh closed the trunk, then sat in the front passenger seat. Donkor pulled away from the curb, moving the car expertly through traffic, weaving back and forth until they entered the road leading out of the airport. At that point he quickly accelerated, leaving April hanging onto the door handle and clutching David's hand.

Minkabh looked back, chuckling. "You'll get used to it. Everyone here drives like this. It seems a little erratic, but there is a system to it."

"That's good to know." April tried to smile.

As they moved along, April was amazed at the sheer size and density of the city. Glass-and-steel hotels and office buildings stood side-by-side with Victorian villas of brick and limestone, and tree-lined side streets meandered off into shade all along the main road.

"It reminds me of Paris," April said.

Minkabh nodded. "Yes. In many ways, this is a European city." He glanced in the rearview mirror. "When were you in Paris?"

"Two years ago—for my work."

Minkabh shook his head. "A shame to spend time there on business."

April smiled. "Well, I did manage a day at the Louvre. And another day at Chartres Cathedral."

"Very good. If you like art, we have excellent museums here as well. Also much fine architecture."

"The domes over there are beautiful."

"That is the Muslim influence—very strong here. Cairo is known as the City of a Thousand Mosques."

"Where are the pyramids?" David asked.

"Straight ahead, but on the west side of the river—the Nile, of course. I will be pleased to take you there in a day or two, after you've settled in."

"That's very kind of you."

"Not at all. I will be your personal tour guide." Minkabh smiled broadly, showing his large white teeth. "And if you wish to explore the city on your own, the metro is very good. But Donkor here is also at your service; you have only to call him. Yes, Donkor?"

The driver nodded. "With pleasure."

"Thank you," David said. "That's far more than anyone could expect."

"We are glad to provide this service for you. I would offer to let you use another car—the Cadillac, for instance—but it would probably not be wise for you to drive in the city."

After a pause, David asked, "I don't mean to be rude, but what do you do for a living?"

Minkabh roared with laughter. "I? I do whatever I like. My grand-father and great-grandfather were collectors of antiquities, and they made a considerable fortune selling items from the tombs to wealthy European visitors. Of course, such practice is now considered looting and is no longer allowed. But my family and I still enjoy the lingering benefits of their illicit trade." He smiled contentedly.

"And are you a collector too? Legally, of course."

"Oh, yes, in an amateur way. In fact, it is my passion."

Donkor turned onto one of the side streets, and April nudged David. "Look at the mansions."

"This area is called Garden City," Minkabh said. "Many wealthy families live here. It is also home to several schools and government agencies. The American embassy is just a block from here—easy access for you, David."

Donkor pulled up to a tall, wrought-iron gate spanning a wide driveway. The gate swung open automatically, and the car glided along a spacious lane lined with palm trees and flowers.

"And here we are," Minkabh said.

April pressed the button to roll down her window, then breathed in the fragrant garden air. "This is beautiful."

"Thank you. I hope you will enjoy your stay here."

After Donkor helped them out of the car and unloaded their bags from the trunk, Minkabh motioned for David and April to enter the house. April could hardly take her eyes off the tall, ornate villa, which was built of reddish-brown stone in art deco style. Many of the windows sported wrought-iron balconies and flower boxes, and the roof was studded with cornices and towers. The large front doors were painted blue with ornate white trimming, giving them an Arabic feel.

"Please," Minkabh said. "Come in and meet my family."

At this, the doors opened, and a woman wearing an elegant red-and-gold *djellaba* stepped out onto the wide, sheltered porch. A little girl, five or six years old, peered around the door frame, her dark eyes wide and her finger in her mouth.

"April, David—may I present my wife, Sharifa, and my daughter, Kakra."

"It's a pleasure to meet you," David said.

"Such a beautiful daughter!" April gushed. She bent over and motioned for the girl to come out, but Kakra just drew farther back behind the door frame.

"Kakra?" David said. "That means 'twin,' doesn't it?"

"Yes," Minkabh said quietly. "But we will tell you that story later."

Lunch was served at a wrought-iron table on a covered patio in back of the villa. The food was simple but delicious—tabouli with lettuce leaves and pita bread, served with a sweet drink April couldn't identify. "This is very good—what is it?" she asked.

"Karkaday," Sharifa said. "Hibiscus."

"The flower?" April looked curiously at the deep-red liquid.

"Yes. We steep the petals in hot water, then add sugar and chill. We also have fruit drinks in the kitchen; if you're ever thirsty—or hungry—just ask one of the servants. And we have plenty of bottled water.

You should never drink the local water here, not even to brush your teeth. The germs will make you sick."

"I read about that," David said.

"But you can buy juice and fruit almost anywhere in the city," Sharifa continued. "And the cooked food at the stands is also okay. Walking in the city is very safe—even for you, April, as long as you dress modestly, as you are now."

April blushed, looking down at her blue pants and lacy white top. "I noticed lots of policemen on the way from the airport."

"Yes," Minkabh said. "That's *why* it's so safe."

After more conversation and a dessert of raspberry ice, Minkabh said, "Your room is on the third floor—in fact, the entire floor is yours. There are quite a few stairs to climb, but it will give you privacy. Your bags are already in your room."

"Thanks for your thoughtfulness," David said.

"Of course. And feel free to come and go as you please. Our home is your home—at least while you're here in Egypt." Minkabh smiled.

David turned to April. "What do you think?"

"I think I need a nap."

Minkabh nodded. "Now would be a good time for a rest. But I advise you not to sleep too long. If you can stay awake until tonight, the jet lag will be much less, and you'll feel better tomorrow."

After lunch, Minkabh showed them their room, which was really more of a suite, complete with a large bedroom and bathroom, a sitting room with a television, and a library, the walls punctuated with tall windows and lined with hundreds of books, many bound in ornately decorated leather. The library also had a desk with a computer, a study table, a couch, and several dark leather reading chairs. "Nice," David whispered to April.

"Too bad you won't be spending much time in here."

"Well, not until I have to go to work."

"And don't you forget it. Until next week, you're *mine*."

David looked at her stoically. "Marriage requires such sacrifice."

CHAPTER 4

O n Tuesday, after a very late breakfast of fried eggs, pastrami, and orange juice, Minkabh spread a large map of Cairo out on the table. "And now," he said, "is there anything in particular you wish to see?"

David and April bent over the map.

"That direction is north," Minkabh said, pointing, then aligning the map, "and we"—he tapped his finger on the paper—"are here. The embassy is very close, just here." He pointed at a small orange square. "The Egyptian Museum is here," he said, moving his finger. "And the pyramids are over here, on the southwest but still very close to the city. And we have shopping, movies, mosques, restaurants—nearly anything you can think of."

David looked at April. "What do you think? Pyramids?"

"I think we should go to the museum first. That way, we'll understand the pyramids better when we see them."

Minkabh clapped David on the shoulder. "Your wife is a wise soul."

"Oh, I know."

"I won't go with you there—you won't need a guide. But Donkor will be glad to drive you."

❧

The museum was nothing like what April had anticipated. It was a creaky old building filled with antiquities piled on dusty antiquities—papyrus scrolls, alabaster jars, tools, boxes, jewelry, statues, coffins, and mummies—including, of course, the famous sarcophagus and golden mask of Pharaoh Tutankhamen. The major exhibits were well-maintained, but many of the display cases seemed outdated and disorganized. In some rooms, ancient treasures were stacked haphazardly against the walls or even stuffed into corners.

April whispered to David, "I hope they don't have a fire in here."

"No kidding. The whole place would go up in seconds."

"It's kind of strange seeing all of this." April paused to look at an unwrapped mummy, its skin darkened by time, its empty eyes mere slits. "These people were alive once. They loved each other and had families. They had hopes and dreams. They wanted to live forever."

David nodded.

"And they ended up as a pile of bones in a glass case, with people looking at them all day long."

"It is a kind of immortality, I guess."

"Not one I'd want."

"Me neither." David peered down at the grinning skull. "Those teeth are particularly nasty."

April laughed.

"Nothing lasts," David said. "Eventually, everything turns to dust."

April looked down at the mummy. "But someday, there'll be a resurrection. Will this actual body come to life again? Or will it happen some other way?"

"I have no idea."

"There's something I've always wondered about: What happens to people who get eaten by sharks? They don't have a body to resurrect."

"I don't suppose we need to worry about that."

April smiled. "Unless we go swimming."

"Very funny. I hear the ocean here is beautiful—so blue you can hardly look at it."

April nodded. "Maybe we should go."

"What about those sharks?"

"Or maybe not."

They moved on to another case, this one containing a large wooden sarcophagus. A printed sign explained some of the writing painted on its surface.

"Look," David said. "The cartouche gives the mummy's name—Hatshepsut."

"You can read that?"

David grinned. "Sure. The sign's printed in plain English."

April laughed, then studied the ancient characters. They were finely done, brushed onto the coffin's surface in thick black ink. "Had a chance to get back to the book of Abraham yet?" she asked.

"No. *Someone* wouldn't let me, remember?"

"That's *right*."

"But we should be having family scripture study, don't you think?"

April nodded. "Yes, we should."

"We could read it together."

"Hmmm. I guess I could stand a little more of your company."

❧

That night, snuggled together in the large, fluffy bed, they started reading together, taking turns with the verses.

"'The Book of Abraham,'" David intoned deeply. "'Translated from the papyrus, by Joseph Smith.'"

"You might try reading with your regular voice," April said.

"This is serious stuff," he replied. But then he started reading naturally. "'A Translation of some ancient Records, that have fallen into our hands from the catacombs of Egypt.—The writings of Abraham while he was in Egypt, called the Book of Abraham, written by his own hand, upon papyrus.'"

"So was it the book that was written by his own hand, or the papyrus?" April looked thoughtful.

"Uh, the book, I guess. Does anyone know the age of the papyrus?"

"Probably." April paused. "Parts of it are in the Church Historical Library, you know."

"Really? Can we see them?"

"I've heard that getting permission takes a long time."

"What if you know someone who works there? Hint, hint."

April shook her head. "Sorry. There's probably not much I can do to speed that one along. I can make the request, though. But the papyri have been published lots of times—I'll help you find some of the books."

"We could check here on the Internet," David suggested.

"We could. But right now we're studying the scriptures, remember?"

David looked at her solemnly. "I'm just waiting for you. It's your turn to read. You're the one holding things up."

April rolled her eyes, then began. "'Chapter 1. In the land of the Chaldeans, at the residence of my fathers, I, Abraham, saw that it was needful for me to obtain another place of residence.'"

"Well, we've certainly done that," David said.

"For now. But when we get home, we'll need to get our own place."

"Why? Don't you like my apartment?"

"Not really." She wrinkled her nose. "It has a sort of old-man smell."

"Old-man smell? And I suppose that doesn't blend well with your old-woman smell?"

April sniffed. "There's no need to be insulting. And besides, it's your turn to read."

David cleared his throat and went on. "'And, finding there was greater happiness and peace and rest for me, I sought for the blessings of the fathers, and the right whereunto I should be ordained to administer the same; having been myself a follower of righteousness, desiring also to be one who possessed great knowledge, and to be a greater follower of righteousness, and to possess a greater knowledge . . .'"

He paused. "Sounds like Abraham wanted everything."

"Everything important."

"He wanted happiness and peace and rest."

"He wanted the priesthood," April said.

"And he wanted great knowledge."

"But after that, he wanted *greater* knowledge—and *greater* righteousness." She paused. "What's the difference between great knowledge and greater knowledge?"

"I don't know. But I'd like to find out."

"Maybe we should stick with *basic* knowledge—at least for now."

"Line upon line," David said.

"Exactly. So keep reading."

David paused. "Hold on. We didn't look at the picture yet. It's part of the story too."

"You're right."

Together they pored over the facsimile at the beginning of the book.

"It looks like some of the papyri in the museum." David pointed at the figures under the altar.

"From what we saw today, I'd say it's an embalming scene. The priest is getting ready to cut out the dead man's organs and put them in the four canopic jars under the table."

"But the caption says this is Abraham fastened on an altar. So did Joseph Smith have this wrong?" David furrowed his brow.

"I don't know. But I do see a couple of interesting things."

"What?"

"The man on the altar has clothes on, so he's not being embalmed. He also has his hands raised." April turned the book on its side so the man was in a standing position. "He's praying."

"Which means he isn't dead."

"Right. There's more going on here than an embalming scene."

"Wow. What about all these names—*Elkenah, Libnah, Mahmackrah,* and *Korash?* What about *Raukeeyang, Shaumau,* and *Shaumahyeem?*"

"We should ask Minkabh." April yawned.

"Do you think he'd know?"

"Maybe. But right now, I think I'm ready to sleep." She smiled and closed her eyes.

※

The next morning at breakfast, David brought out his triple combination.

"You have a book," Minkabh said.

"Yes. We thought you might be able to answer some questions for us." David opened to the book of Abraham and handed it to their host. "It looks like an embalming scene, but some things don't quite fit."

Minkabh took the book. "You're right." He scrutinized the page. "The priest should have the head of a jackal to represent Anubis, god of mummification and guide of the dead. The bird on the right should have a human head, not that of a hawk, to represent the dead man's soul—his *ba*." Minkabh paused. "Why is this man wearing shoes?"

David laughed. "We were hoping *you* could tell *us*."

"Perhaps it shows he is walking away. See, he has one foot in front of the other."

"And is he praying?"

"Yes, he is. Very good. This is unusual."

"What about the names under the picture?"

Minkabh scanned the captions. "Only one of these names is Egyptian—*Korash*. It is the same as *Cyrus* in Persian."

David's face fell. He looked over at April.

"All the others are Hebrew," Minkabh said. "*Elkenah* means 'God has created'—the *El* part means 'God.' *Libnah* refers to the moon—it means 'white.' *Mahmackrah* . . ." He shook his head. "That one I do not know. *Raukeeyang* means 'expanse.' *Shaumau* means 'high' or 'lofty.' And *Shaumahyeem* is the plural of *Shaumau*, so it means something like 'the heavens.' Usually the last syllable would be spelled 'im,' but the pronunciation is the same."

Now David was smiling. "Very impressive. Where did you learn all that?"

"I told you—antiquities are my passion. I would be happy to help you with such things anytime. But what is this book about Father Abraham?"

"It's a book published by our church."

Minkabh smiled. "Yes, you are Mormons, from Utah. But I did not know you were people of the book, as Muslims are."

"We believe in several books. This one is part of our scriptures."

"Then we are brothers. May I read it?"

"Please," David said. "Use my copy. We'll be very interested in hearing what you think."

❦

David and April spent most of the next day relaxing and enjoying each other's company. But when April decided to take a nap in the afternoon, David finally had his chance to explore the villa's library. He crept down the carpeted hall, then turned the shining brass handle on the large oak door, revealing shelf after shelf, volume upon volume, of beautiful, beautiful books. With a satisfied smile, he closed the door behind him. Walking along a wall full of shelves, he ran his fingers over the rich leather bindings, noticing the gold embossing on the spines, smelling the dark odor of ink and paper.

Someday, he thought, *I'm going to have a room just like this one.* But that day, he knew, was a long way off. For now, he'd just have to enjoy what had been placed before him.

The library shelves were arranged by subject—history, language, art, science, and so on. He turned to the language section, wanting to learn more about Hebrew and its possible associations with Egyptian. What he found surprised him. According to several of the books, many of the world's alphabets were originally based on the hieroglyphs of ancient Egypt. With some modifications, the Egyptian characters were used in ancient Hebrew as *aleph*, ox; *beth*, house; *gimel*, throw stick; and so on—which had eventually become modern Hebrew; then Greek *alpha*, *beta*, and *gamma*; and finally English *A*, *B*, and *C*. David found it fascinating that the letters themselves had meaning. There was *vav*, nail; *yodh*, hand; *mem*, water; *resh*, head; *pe*, mouth; and many more.

Especially interesting were the clear similarities between the early Hebrew alphabet and Egyptian hieroglyphics; he could definitely see the connection. And that made perfect sense—after all, the children of Israel had spent hundreds of years as captives in Egypt. Abraham had spent time in Egypt, even teaching the Egyptians the science of astronomy. And his descendant Joseph, who was sold into Egypt as a slave, had eventually become an Egyptian official.

David looked up from his book, staring out the window for a few minutes. *Even Jesus spent time in Egypt,* he thought, remembering the story of how Mary and Joseph had escaped the murderous rampage of King Herod and his soldiers.

David pulled a copy of the Bible from one of the shelves, turned to the book of Matthew, and found the passage he was looking for: "Behold, the angel of the Lord appeareth to Joseph in a dream, saying, Arise, and take the young child and his mother, and flee into Egypt, and be thou there until I bring thee word: for Herod will seek the young child to destroy him. When he arose, he took the young child and his mother by night, and departed into Egypt: And was there until the death of Herod: that it might be fulfilled which was spoken of the Lord by the prophet, saying, Out of Egypt have I called my son."

And now, David thought, *here I am.* But would Egypt be a place of safety for him, as it was for the Savior? What experiences would be waiting for him when he started work in just a few short days? He thought of April sleeping in the bedroom down the hall, and his worries disappeared. Instead, he felt happy and secure. *Surely,* he thought, *everything will be just fine.*

Egypt was hot as a furnace, as a refiner's fire; even the Nile breezes creeping through Cairo made little difference. But the men were meeting anyway, in a private room at the back at a coffeehouse near Orabi Square.

"We should have met in the park," one of the men said. "It's stifling in here." He slurped his coffee, then lit a cigarette, blowing the smoke through his nose.

"There's no tea at the park," a smaller man replied, taking a sip from a tiny brass cup.

"You and your tea."

"You and your cigarettes. Why do you not smoke the *shisha,* like a civilized man?"

"Enough." Baruti Massri, the group's leader, clapped his hands. "We're here on business. You can finish your infantile bickering later." He smoothed back his thick white hair, then looked around the circle, frowning. "Where's Runihura?"

The men looked around at each other, keeping silent.

"Late, it seems," the smoker finally said. He took another puff, inhaling deeply.

"As usual. We will begin without him."

"He is a madman anyway," the little man said.

Instantly, Baruti raised his voice in anger. "He is *useful.* Are you willing to give what he will give?"

The man lowered his eyes. "If it comes to that."

Baruti nodded. "And so it may—as it did with our associate Abasi."

The man sipping tea looked up. "The attack on the ambassador's mansion was foolish. Already they are increasing security at the embassy."

"Foolish?" Baruti said. "You understand nothing. As men of honor, we gave the Americans a fair warning to leave our country—a warning they have chosen to ignore. Now they will pay the price." He turned to a large man, previously silent, dressed in white and sitting back from the circle. "Minkabh, what news on the visas?"

The big man cleared his throat. "Both good and bad. Many of the visas have been cleared at the embassy. When the rest are accepted, our agents can join the others in America."

"And all is ready in America?"

"Yes. Our attacks will be sudden—and devastating."

"And the bad news?"

Minkabh paused. "The FBI has been called in to investigate the embassy. They are watching, so we must move slowly and carefully. But we will get the other visas through."

"You are a cautious man—maybe too cautious. Some might even wonder whose side you are on." Baruti narrowed his eyes.

"I have spent many years building my relationship with the Americans. I refuse to throw that away for the sake of a few days."

"One of these agents is staying with you, I understand."

"Yes—and his wife."

"Good. That will give you leverage. You must get this man out of the way so the visas can be cleared before the bombing takes place."

"I will. But I must be subtle. The Americans look on me as a friend, and it would not do to destroy that illusion. This will take time."

Runihura joined the group, settling his skinny frame into a chair by the door. "Time?" he said. "Left to you, it will take years."

Minkabh glared. "You dare lecture me? You, who are always late?"

Runihura shrugged.

"If I push too hard, our plans will come to nothing. This is a delicate operation."

"You are overly worried," Runihura said. "But soon it will not matter—the embassy will be destroyed. Then the attacks in America will drive the point home, on their own soil. Perhaps then the Americans will keep to their own business."

The men nodded in agreement.

"So may it be," Baruti said, smoothing his white hair. "So may it be."

The following day was the Muslim Sabbath, so things were quiet around the villa as Minkabh and his family went to the mosque and attended to their religious duties. The newlyweds spent some time on the computer in the library looking for a Latter-day Saint meeting they could attend in or near Cairo, but even the official Church Web site had no listing for such a thing. So David and April decided to have their own meeting.

With the rest of the household gone, they met in the villa library, sitting at the big study table, both feeling a little silly at the formality of the occasion with just the two of them present. Still, April gave a heartfelt opening prayer and then read a verse from Matthew: "Where two or three are gathered together in my name, there am I in the midst of them." They tried to sing "Jesus, Once of Humble Birth," but neither one could remember the words, so they stumbled through it together as best they could, smiling at their largely unsuccessful effort.

After the song, David blessed the sacrament—two broken bits of bread and a bottle of water—and passed it to April, who took some and then solemnly passed it back to David. Neither one wanted to give a "talk," so they ended up expressing their love for each other and talking about the things they were grateful for; it ended up being a testimony meeting as much as anything else.

Finally, David gave the closing prayer, asking for help and protection for both of them. The experience was as sweet as any they'd experienced anywhere, and, for that brief time, they felt almost as though the angels were watching over them, foreigners and strangers in a very strange land.

CHAPTER 5

On Saturday Minkabh took David and April to see the pyramids. Donkor drove the big, black Mercedes over the bridge and swiftly through the city, stopping after a surprisingly short time at the pyramid complex.

"Wow, they're huge!" David said, scrambling out of the car. He opened the door for April, and together they admired the ancient monuments towering over the plain.

Minkabh joined them, leaning against the car. "The Great Pyramid is the last of the Seven Wonders of the Ancient World," he said. "It was finished in 2650 B.C. and for 3,800 years was the tallest building in the world."

"You really are a tour guide," David said.

Minkabh laughed. "I'll try not to be the professor. But if you have questions, I'll be happy to answer them."

"Can we go inside?" David asked.

"Yes. But first we have other business to attend to." Minkabh gestured toward April, who had trudged off over the sand and was making arrangements for a camel ride.

David shook his head, then shouted at April, "I thought we were coming to see the pyramids."

"*I* thought we were coming to have fun," she shouted back.

Minkabh waved his arms. "Wait, wait!" he yelled. "They will cheat you, they will cheat you!" He looked at David. "The camel drivers are notorious for taking advantage of tourists. But never mind—I will make the arrangements." He strode off over the sand.

David had never been on a camel before, and the sensation was a little like riding a horse—on stilts. April sat behind him, her arms around his waist, hanging on for dear life, although there was really not much danger; the camels were strung together with ropes, and the camel drivers rode in front or walked alongside the slowly moving caravan, making sure that nothing went wrong. And, as it turned out, the newlyweds *did* see the pyramids—the camels went completely around the complex, with one of the drivers shouting out comments about various points of interest.

David was particularly taken with the Sphinx. It was much smaller than the pyramids, but its enigmatic face seemed to peer through time, staring across the desert, over the river, and off to the eastern horizon, making David wonder what it had seen during its lifetime of more than four thousand years.

As the caravan started to return to the parking lot, David noticed Minkabh, still near the Mercedes, talking with a small, dark man, who was gesturing wildly, flailing his skinny arms in the air. Minkabh was leaning forward, pushing the man's chest with his index finger over and over again, forcefully making some kind of point. When the man noticed the camels, he threw up his hands, turned, and jumped into a small blue sports car, then roared away into the distance.

As Minkabh came to help David and April down from their camel, David noticed the tightness of his lips, the red anger behind his dark skin. "Is something wrong?" David stepped down onto the sand, then turned to help April. "Was that man giving you some kind of trouble?"

"No, no," Minkabh said. "He is a business associate, trying to sell me some cylinder seals. I told him I wasn't interested—to me, they look like forgeries."

"He looked pretty upset."

Minkabh looked up the road out of the parking lot. "He is a fool. He lets his feelings get in the way of his business—something I try not to do."

David nodded.

"But let us think of better things," Minkabh said with a sweep of his arms. "Let us explore the Great Pyramid of Giza."

❧

To David's disappointment, the passage into the pyramid was extraordinarily ordinary: a square, sloping tunnel without decoration, without hieroglyphics, without much of anything but stone and dust. The air was stale, but at least the thick stone walls provided some relief from the sweltering heat outside. Illuminated by sporadic electric lights, the passage led—after a very long walk—into the King's Chamber, which was completely empty except for a roughly carved stone sarcophagus, which itself was empty.

David helped April into the chamber, then turned to Minkabh. "This was built as a tomb, right?" The words echoed dully in the barren room.

Minkabh nodded. "Yes. And yet, it is empty. Perhaps the pharaoh was resurrected." He smiled wryly. "But it is more likely that millennia ago his remains turned to dust."

"Why isn't the tomb decorated? I was expecting something amazing, like the tomb of King Tut."

"When it was first built, it probably was decorated," Minkabh said. "The walls would have been covered with writing and pictures, painted in rich colors, and the chamber would have been filled with objects the pharaoh would need in the afterlife. But only a few years after his burial, all of that was looted."

"Really?"

"Yes. There were looters in antiquity, just as there are today. They took everything of value, and over the centuries the wind and sand have done the rest. It is actually quite rare to find an undisturbed tomb. The King Tuts of the world are few indeed."

"Were there really traps to catch looters?"

Minkabh smiled. "You mean like in *Indiana Jones?*"

David nodded.

"Actually, yes—falling rocks, holes in the floor, that sort of thing. Unexplored tombs can be dangerous."

April spoke up. "Are there other chambers in the pyramid that haven't been found yet?"

"Undoubtedly. But the authorities are understandably reluctant to have people boring holes into what has become a world treasure." He smiled. "But if you're interested in seeing how it might have looked, I know a special place we can visit. It's not far—just a few kilometers on the other side of the river, near the Muqattam Hills."

David looked at April. "Let's go!"

❧

"This," Minkabh said as the car slowed near an ancient stone wall, "is the Necropolis—the City of the Dead."

Through the window, David could see dozens of tall, domed

structures, some with towers like a mosque. Many were decorated with enamel and gold leaf. He also noticed the stench of decay. As they passed into the "city," David was surprised at the number of people walking about. In the doorways and under porches, people were talking, trading, even cooking over charcoal fires. In the dusty street, boys were playing some kind of ball game, the two teams hollering and running from one side of the road to the other.

"Why is it called the City of the Dead?" April asked. She wrinkled her nose, then covered it with her hand.

Minkabh sighed. "It is an interesting thing. The buildings you see here are crypts—the resting place of emirs and sultans. But there is an ancient custom that families must stay forty days with the body of a loved one. The poor stay in tents or shanties, but many wealthy families have built not just crypts but whole houses as part of a crypt. Many houses are hundreds of years old."

"So are these people staying here until the forty days are up?" April asked.

"No. There is a housing shortage in Cairo, and even though it is illegal, the people you see actually live here, in these gigantic tombs. They have nowhere else to go." Minkabh nodded toward the children playing in the street. "Look closely."

David watched the children running back and forth, striking a ball with sticks in a kind of dusty hockey match. The ball was misshapen; it looked like a volleyball with dark holes. And then David realized: they were batting around a human skull, and some of the sticks appeared to be leg bones. He nudged April. "I see it," she said.

Minkabh shrugged. "Most people don't come here. They think of it as cursed or haunted."

"I can see why," David said.

"But this is not what I brought you to see. Please, let us go on, and I will show you a much older burial complex."

As the car moved on, David noticed that April could hardly take her eyes from the window. "Is something wrong?" he asked.

"I just wonder about these people. How can they live here? Do they have enough to eat?"

"Many do not," Minkabh said. "Although some have jobs in the city. But in many ways, it is actually a good place. The people share what they have, and they look after each other. There is a wealth of human life, even here, among the dead."

April turned to David. "We should come back. Maybe we could help in some way."

David nodded. "Maybe so."

They continued to drive past the tombs, beyond the lush border of the Nile, and out into the desert. A few minutes later, they came to a bend in the road, and the car pulled up to a circle of long, rocky hills that curved out across the barren plain.

"So close to the city?" David asked.

Minkabh nodded. "Remember, the whole city was once a domain of ancient Egypt. Even downtown construction workers continue to find fragments of the past."

As David got out of the car, he noticed a chain-link fence topped with barbed wire and a closed gate from which hung a large gray padlock. Above the lock was a yellow sign in Arabic and English: "Danger! Radioactive waste. Keep out!"

"We can't go in there!" David said.

Minkabh smiled grimly. "Don't worry; things are not always as they seem." He stepped up to the gate, pulled some keys from his pocket, and opened the lock. "I have special privileges here," he said, raising his dark eyebrows. "Friends in high places." He swung the gate open so David and April could enter, then closed and locked it from the inside. "This is a burial complex, discovered in 2004 but kept secret from the public. It, too, is a city of the dead, but it is much older than the one we just saw." He paused. "It seems that people have been burying their dead outside of Cairo for nearly five thousand years."

Minkabh walked farther along the side of the hill, stopping at a rough wooden door fastened to posts with new aluminum hinges. He swung the door open, then retrieved several expensive-looking flashlights that were stored in metal hangers on the back of the door. "With any luck," he said, "the batteries should still be good. I replaced them not long ago." He pressed the switch, and the light shone brightly. He took a step inside the doorway, then down a few steps into the darkness, motioning for David and April to follow. "Behold!" he said dramatically. "The tombs of ancient Egypt."

CHAPTER 6

"There are actually twenty tombs in this complex," Minkabh said, shining his flashlight into a passage leading off to the left of the main chamber in which he, David, and April were standing. "The objects from twelve of the tombs have already been removed for study, and eventually they'll be placed in the Cairo Museum. But for now, I can show you what's left—although you must promise not to touch anything."

David and April nodded.

"Also, you must promise to stay with me. The burial complex is huge, with many rooms and passageways, and you could easily become lost without a guide."

"I can't believe you'd even bring us down here," David said. "Thanks for doing this."

Minkabh shrugged. "I believe you are trustworthy people. And besides, there are things here that you might find interesting—based on your book of Abraham."

"You've been reading the book?" David asked.

"Yes. Not everything fits with my understanding, but some things do—and those are the things I'd like to show you." To David's surprise, Minkabh pulled out David's triple combination, then thumbed rapidly through the pages.

"And now," Minkabh said, his eyes sparkling, "I will read to you." He cleared his throat and began: "'I, Abraham, had the Urim and Thummim, which the Lord my God had given unto me, in Ur of the Chaldees; and I saw the stars, that they were very great, and that one of them was nearest unto the throne of God; and there were many great ones which were near unto it.'" Minkabh paused, then threw his flashlight beam up onto the ceiling. "What do you see?"

To David's amazement, the tomb's ceiling was filled with stars, painted in white and outlined against a deep blue background.

"The ancient Egyptians were very interested in astronomy; they were experts on the study of the heavenly bodies. In fact, some of the passageways in the Great Pyramid were cut to align precisely with certain stars that the Egyptians considered important. Here, for example," Minkabh said, moving his flashlight, "we see a representation of the constellation Orion; over here is the Big Dipper. All of these had significance in the Egyptians' ideas of the afterlife. So when your book talks about the stars having 'times and seasons in the revolutions thereof' and says that Abraham was 'reasoning upon the principles of astronomy in the king's court,' it makes perfect sense."

Minkabh resumed reading. "'And he said unto me: This is Shinehah, which is the sun. And he said unto me: Kokob, which is star. And he said unto me: Olea, which is the moon. And he said unto me: Kokaubeam, which signifies stars, or all the great lights, which were in the firmament of heaven.'

"Now, *Shinehah* literally means 'year.' *Kokob* means 'star,' just as the book says. *Oleah* is *Yareah,* 'moon.' And *Kokaubeam* is 'stars'—the plural of *kokob.* But that 'eam' ending should really be spelled 'im.'

And that means—what? Do you remember?" He tilted his head, like a teacher waiting for a response.

"It means the words are Hebrew," David said.

"Exactly—just as we saw before." Minkabh raised his chin. "So what you have here is a Jewish book, not an Egyptian one—although it is presented in an Egyptian form. So as you study, keep that in mind; you'll understand it better."

"All right."

"And now, let us press farther into the tombs." Minkabh turned, leading David and April through a low doorway and down a straight, square passage.

As they walked, David noticed that the floor, walls, and ceiling were built of immense blocks of solid stone, and occasionally trickles of dust and sand would fall from the cracks over their heads.

"Is there any danger of the ceiling caving in?" he asked.

"If we had an earthquake, yes. In 1992 a quake in Cairo killed nearly four hundred people. It started just a few miles from the pyramids, but they held together. The Egyptians were excellent builders."

I sure hope so, David thought. He took hold of April's hand.

After navigating through several more sequences of narrow passages and dark doorways, Minkabh paused. "Howard Carter was the famous discoverer of the tomb of Pharaoh Tutankhamen," he said. "After making a hole in the door of the unopened crypt, he held up a candle and looked inside. What he saw so astonished him that he was unable to speak. Finally, Lord Carnarvon, his financier, asked, 'Can you see anything?' And Carter answered, 'Yes, wonderful things.'"

Minkabh pushed on a large stone slab, which swung slowly open into a dark chamber. "Now, what do you see?" His flashlight beam revealed a glint of gold in the midst of the darkness.

As David and April turned their lights into the shadows, they saw gleaming treasures everywhere—golden chariots, statues of gold and ebony, a fleet of miniature ships to accommodate the deceased on his trip to the netherworld, a throne of gold, precious jewelry, and much more. Every corner, every niche of this time capsule from the ancient world was filled with objects of immeasurable value. And in the center of the room, surrounded by all this magnificence, was a coffin of solid gold—surely the resting place of an Egyptian king who had lain for centuries in darkness, in the unfathomable silence of the ancient tomb.

For many seconds, no one spoke. Finally, April stuttered out, "It's—it's magnificent."

"Indeed it is," Minkabh said. "But there's one thing in particular I want to show you." He ducked his head and stepped into the chamber, with David and April close behind. As they moved to the head of the coffin, suddenly David stood stock-still.

"It's an altar," he said. "Exactly like the one in the book of Abraham."

"This is what I brought you here to see," Minkabh said. He crouched at the side of the gleaming object. "Another one, exactly like this, was found in the tomb of King Tut. It is a couch, fashioned from gold and decorated with the head of a lion at each corner. It was used as a table for mummification and probably, on occasion, as a sacrificial altar, just as your book describes. See, here are grooves to channel the blood." He ran his flashlight over the sides of the altar.

"So Abraham could have been tied to a couch like this one?" David asked.

"Yes—but this is the interesting thing. There is an ancient tradition that Abraham was to be offered as a sacrifice, but not on an altar. Rather, he was to be thrown into a fiery furnace, like the prophet Daniel."

David nodded. "But isn't the sacrifice killed before it's burned?"

Minkabh raised a finger. "Yes, that's a good point. Perhaps that is what is meant. If so, then your book is quite accurate—it certainly fits the ancient traditions. Or perhaps Abraham was to be *burned* on the altar. The picture shows a knife, but that is never mentioned in the text—only the fact that he was to be sacrificed."

"Interesting," David said. "I guess I hadn't noticed that."

Minkabh stood, wiping the dust from his hands. "There is much more we could see here, but perhaps this is enough for one day. We've been gone a long time, and dinner will be waiting for us at the villa."

"Thanks again," David said. "This has been great."

⁂

That night, after dinner, David and April went to bed early, exhausted from their long day of sightseeing. For several minutes, they simply relaxed, breathing softly, their eyes closed. Then David turned onto his side, looking over at April. "Wow, what a day."

"Mmm-hmm," she mumbled sleepily.

"I *said,* 'Wow, what a day.'"

April opened one eye. "And *I* said, 'Mmm-hmm.' But I'd *like* to go to sleep, if you don't mind."

David rolled onto his back, staring up at the ceiling. "Wasn't that just the most incredible experience?" He let out a sigh.

"Mmm. Those camels *were* a lot of fun." She gave the blankets a tug, pulling them up to her chin.

"Ha, ha. You know that's not what I meant."

April smiled. "Yeah, I know."

"So did you enjoy our honeymoon?" He leaned over and kissed her on the cheek.

"Very much. I'm sorry you have to go to work tomorrow—especially since it's Sunday."

"Yeah, me too."

"At least I'll be here for you to come home to."

David nodded. "I'm so glad we can be here together."

April put her hand behind his neck and pulled his face close to hers. "It can still be our honeymoon; we just won't be together as much." Gently, she kissed him. Then she pulled back, looking into his eyes. "You be careful."

"I will. But I also need to be aggressive—Wilcox specifically told me that. And I need that promotion—I have a wife to support."

"True. And I *will* be needing some of the finer things." She smiled. "Just make sure you're there to enjoy them with me."

David nodded. "Do you think I'll do okay?"

"Of course." She put her hand on his cheek, looking directly into his eyes. "Of course you will. Just be yourself and do the best job you can. That's all anyone can ask."

David nodded. "I know," he said. But he wondered if that would really be enough. Two hours later, he was still thinking about it. But he needed to stop, to focus. He had a job to do. And with that decision, he fell asleep.

PART 2

CHAPTER 7

Sunday morning, as David walked through the large glass doors at the embassy, he was greeted by an olive-skinned young woman with short, dark hair. Dressed in a white blouse with a gray skirt and jacket, she looked every inch the American official—but her deep-red lips gave her face a sensuous quality that David found disarming.

Putting out her hand, she said, "I'm Agent Pam Lawford. You must be Agent Hunter. I've been waiting for you. It's a pleasure to meet you."

"Uh . . . ," he managed to get out. "I . . ."

"Are you all right?" she tilted her head, a slight smile on her face.

"Sorry. I just . . ." He coughed. "I guess I'm a little nervous."

"Well, that's only natural."

"So, um, where are you from?" David asked.

"New York City." Her eyes twinkled.

"No kidding?"

"Yup. It's a great place." She put her hand on his arm. "You should visit sometime."

David wasn't sure if she meant the city in general or herself in particular, but he decided he'd better not push it. "So what's going on here?"

"Oh, you'll see; I'll give you the full report. But for now, come with me. I'll show you our office." She turned and started walking down the hall, her high heels clicking confidently on the tile floor.

Hoo, boy, David thought. *It's a good thing I'm married.* He looked at his wedding ring, and in his mind's eye, he could see April, her arms folded, her face grim. *"And don't you forget it!"* she seemed to say. David let out his breath, then followed Pam down a series of stairs and into a tiny room in the basement.

"This is home," she said.

"Not much to look at, is it."

"Nope. But it'll have to do. So far, I've been observing people and taking notes, and I'm thinking you might want to help tabulate my findings."

David lifted his chin. "Are you in charge here?"

"I don't think either of us is 'in charge.' We're partners." She shrugged. "But I've already been here a week, so I'm starting to get a pretty good idea of what's going on."

David nodded. "Sorry. I didn't mean for us to get off on the wrong foot."

"It's all right. Maybe it would help if I filled you in."

"Sounds good," David said, taking a seat.

"The main problem is that visas are being issued to people who shouldn't be getting them—and turned down for people who should."

"When you say 'people who shouldn't be getting them,' you mean terrorists, right?"

"Exactly. The workers may not always *know* they're terrorists, but they're also not trying very hard to find out. They're not screening people the way they should. In some cases, I think the workers *do* know who the terrorists are and are letting them through anyway."

"And if they get to America . . ."

"That's right. *Boom!*"

David whistled.

"They need to be stopped, but just keeping an eye on people makes them cautious. They know if they're caught, their plans will be jeopardized. Just the fact that we're here is a deterrent, especially since we'll be monitoring the visas that go through. Supposedly that's a secret, but I've leaked it to enough people that everyone must know by now."

"That should slow them down. But can't we just fire the people who are causing the problems?"

Pam shook her head. "I'm afraid it's not that simple. Some of these people have political connections. Others *want* to do the right thing but are under constant pressure not to. And all of the illegal activity is difficult to *prove,* but that's what we're going to have to do to get these people out of here. I know what I've seen, and I believe I know who the main suspects are, but we'll need to gather solid evidence that we can present to the powers-that-be."

"Okay," David said. "In other words, we need to record phone conversations, intercept letters and e-mail—that kind of thing."

"Exactly. And keep monitoring what's going on. How good are you at hacking into a computer system?"

Smiling, David stretched his arms over his head. "One of my favorite things."

"Good—because I don't have a clue."

"Sounds like we'll make a good team, then."

Pam smiled, her dark eyes flashing. "I think you might be right."

Runihura Badawi threw open the back door of the old school bus, now painted green, with "Badawi Landscaping" stenciled in black on both sides. He'd torn out and sold the banks of seats, and the bus was now stuffed to the windows with bags of rocks and sacks full of fertilizer—"Ammonium Nitrate," according to the lettering.

"Give me a hand with these, will you?" Runihura said to the worker at the salvage yard. He pulled himself up with his skinny arms, got his footing inside the bus, then turned around. "Come, help me load the barrels."

The worker started handing up the fifty-gallon drums, his gray T-shirt stained with sweat on his chest and under his armpits. "What are you going to do with all these?" he grunted.

"Storage," Runihura said. "We have many kinds of landscaping stones, different kinds of fertilizer, and so on. All must be stored separately. These barrels are an economical solution."

"Yes, I see," the worker said.

Several minutes later, after the barrels were loaded, Runihura hopped out of the bus and closed the door. "You're a good worker," he said.

"Thank you," the man said. "Would you like to hire me?"

Runihura hesitated. "I . . . uh . . . I don't know how much longer I'll be in business. Sorry."

"It's all right," the man said.

Runihura walked to the front of the bus, opened the door, and climbed up into the driver's seat. Next, he would drive to a gas station on the outskirts of town and fill the barrels with diesel fuel. He could fill only so many at a time without the seller becoming suspicious, and every day he felt himself becoming more impatient. But soon . . . soon. He closed his eyes. Soon he would have enough fertilizer, fuel, rocks, and barrels to make an enormous car bomb. *A bus bomb, actually,* he thought with satisfaction. *One of the biggest the world has ever seen.* Then perhaps the Americans would mind their own business.

Then perhaps they would go home where they belonged. *Actually,* he thought, *they will have to—if any of them are left. Their embassy will be completely destroyed.*

❧

David threw up his hands in exasperation. The computer in the embassy basement was one of the slowest he'd ever seen, and he was finding it difficult to explore the embassy's network when he had to wait nearly half a second for every keystroke to appear on the screen. The computer was Windows-based, but David preferred working in the command window that most people didn't even know about. He felt that it gave him more hands-on control without having to reach for the mouse every other second. And, since the command window didn't rely on the elaborate Windows interface, it was usually faster. But not on this computer.

He changed directories, then issued a command, scanning the screen for indications of hidden network locations. Right then his e-mail program flashed a notification that he'd received a message. David suspected it was probably from Wilcox. Or maybe April was using the computer back at the villa and wanted to say hello. But when he opened the message, it wasn't from an address he recognized. In fact, the address was being routed from an Internet site that David knew was used for sending e-mail anonymously. He had no idea who might be doing that with a message for him, but the words were certainly clear enough: "Your life is in danger. You must leave Egypt immediately." It was signed "A friend."

You're not going to get rid of me that easily, he thought grimly. But then he paused. Maybe the message was right. Most of the people he'd met at the embassy were none too friendly, so it was certainly possible. But he wasn't ready to quit just yet. After all, he was just getting started.

And besides, he *needed* that promotion. He set his jaw. For now, he'd just have to keep his eyes open. As April had said, he'd need to be careful.

He returned to exploring the network, tapping at the keys, but suddenly the basement office seemed cold and full of shadows. Pam was gone—somewhere upstairs collecting more data—and he couldn't go home for several more hours. Usually he didn't mind being alone, but now he felt almost as if someone were watching him.

He got up and scanned the desk and walls for hidden cameras or microphones, pulling out drawers and looking under the desktop and chairs. He stood on top of the desk and examined the light fixtures. Finally, he took a screwdriver and removed the light-switch and outlet covers. But he didn't find anything unusual—everything looked just as it should.

He went back to the computer, opened the command window, and typed in a string of commands. But suddenly an error message popped up on the screen—"Application error 1471—logger interrupted." David frowned. What did that mean?

He issued a command to find out what processes were running. The listing included his e-mail program, the Windows notepad, a network scanning utility, and various system processes. But at the end of the list was something unusual—an entry for "kybdlggr," which seemed to be locked up. Whatever he'd typed had made that process crash. But David knew what it was. It was a *keyboard logger,* running underneath the Windows system. No wonder the computer was running so slowly! Someone had been recording every keystroke he made. Someone had been watching him.

❧

An hour later, with a broad smile, David put his hands into the air, triumphant. He'd successfully hacked into the inner workings of the embassy's computer system—which meant that now he could do anything he wanted. He could intercept e-mail messages, modify records—whatever was needed to get in the terrorists' way.

And then he had an idea. It should be possible to pull out the names of everyone who had applied for a visa, and then to compare those names with a database of known terrorists—and suspected terrorists. It wouldn't catch them all, of course, since many of the applications would be under false names. But it would probably catch some of them. Certainly, it was worth trying. After that, it would be a simple matter to have them arrested.

Then another idea popped into his mind. He restarted the keyboard logger. Then he tried typing the string of commands he'd entered before. Sure enough, he got the same "logger interrupted" message—which meant that he could turn the logger off and on at will. He could turn it off when he wanted to pull out information and modify records; he could turn it on when he wanted to give the bad guys *disinformation,* to throw them off track. It would be easy to make them think he was doing one thing when he was really doing something else. With a rising sense of excitement, he started in.

"I found a keyboard logger," he told Pam as soon as she returned to the office.

Pam took a seat. "No kidding?"

"Yup."

"So someone in the IT department—"

"Or someone else with access to the computer . . ." David sat back in his chair, leaving the thought unfinished.

"That should be a fairly small group of people. It shouldn't be hard to figure out who it is."

"I think we should let it ride," David said. "We can use it to our advantage."

Pam nodded. "Clever."

"Thanks. I had another idea, too."

"Okay."

"Could you run the names from the visa applications against the terrorist database?"

"David, that's brilliant! I'll get started right now."

Pam turned to her computer. It really was a good idea, she had to admit—very clever of him. But now she had to figure out what to do if she found some matches. She certainly couldn't let David see them. But she also couldn't delete the applications or else the visas wouldn't be issued. The solution, she decided—and, actually, it too was rather brilliant—was to delete any matching terrorists from the database itself.

Too bad about the keyboard logger, she thought. On the other hand, though, now that he'd discovered it, he *thought* he had the upper hand. She supposed it wouldn't be hard to intercept what he was doing and turn it to her own advantage, making the logger itself into a sort of "double agent"—not unlike herself. She smiled at the irony. And, of course, she'd have to see what she could do about distracting David in other ways—something that would be a lot more fun than destroying the integrity of computer records.

After work that night, David and April finally got back to their study of the book of Abraham—this time in the library as a sort of family home evening. But April wasn't happy; David could tell.

"Is something wrong?" he asked.

April shook her head. "No, it's okay."

"Sorry I was so late getting home from work."

April smiled thinly. "I guess the honeymoon's over."

David thought for a moment. "Well, officially I guess it is. But tomorrow I'll try to get home earlier. Okay?"

"Promise?"

"Promise."

"Okay. I'm sure you had a busy day."

"You wouldn't believe. But I accomplished a lot; I figured out a way to help identify terrorists getting visas to the U.S."

"Wow, really?"

"Well, we haven't actually identified them yet, but we will."

She patted his hand. "I'm proud of you. But let's not talk about work now, okay?"

"Okay."

Minkabh still had David's triple combination, so they took turns reading from April's scriptures until they reached Facsimile 2, the second picture in the book.

All of the hieroglyphics in the picture were interesting, but it was figure number 7 that caught David's eye.

"'Represents God sitting upon his throne,'" he read aloud. Together they looked at the picture. "I wonder if that's how the Egyptians thought of it."

"Maybe," April said. "Or at least that was Joseph Smith's interpretation of it."

"Maybe that's why he wrote 'represents.'"

April nodded.

"The god is holding his arm to the square," David said.

"And see the shape over his hand?"

"Wow."

"'Revealing through the heavens the grand Key-words of the

Priesthood,'" April read. She paused. "I'm starting to see why the temple worker said we should study the book of Abraham."

"What's the bird doing?" David asked.

"It's 'the sign of the Holy Ghost unto Abraham, in the form of a dove.'"

"Right. But what's it *doing?*"

April looked at the picture. "It has one hand raised, and the other hand is holding something."

David paused. "One of those Egyptian eyes."

"It's called a *wedjat-eye*," she said confidently. "It's also known as the Eye of the Moon or the Eye of Ra."

"But Ra is the sun. So which is it, moon or sun?"

"It depends. If it's a left eye, it's the moon. If it's a right eye, it's the sun."

"Well, I'm impressed."

"Actually, David, I'm surprised you didn't know that." She fluttered her eyelashes and then laughed.

David rolled his eyes. "Someone's been studying while I've been at work."

"You betcha." April nodded. "I've been learning a lot. I need something to fill my lonely hours."

"What about *my* lonely hours?"

"You don't have lonely hours. You spend all day with your partner, Pam."

David blushed. "Strictly business, I'll have you know."

She kissed him on the cheek. "I know." Then she tilted her head. "So, is she pretty?"

"Well, uh . . ."

April narrowed her eyes. "I'll take that as a yes."

"Let's just say she's not nearly as pretty as you."

"Good answer," April said.

"And time to change the subject." David pointed at the picture. "What's this little thing at the bottom of figure 7?"

April pulled the page closer. "I don't know. But it looks like it's praying—both hands are raised, like Abraham in Facsimile 1."

"Why did they do that?"

April shrugged. "Maybe to get attention, like raising your hand in school. Maybe it's a way of saying, 'Hey, look at me; I want to say something.'"

"Could be." David looked more closely at the tiny figure. "Is that supposed to be a person?"

"I have no idea."

He pulled the computer over. "Let's see what Google says." After a little searching, they found a commentary on the book of Abraham. Together they read the words on the screen:

> *God sitting upon his throne:* A seated ithyphallic god holding aloft a flail. This is a form of Min, the god of the regenerative, procreative forces of nature, combined with Horus, as the hawk's tail indicates.
>
> Before the god is what appears to be a bird holding an eye. This could symbolize the *ba,* or soul (which the Egyptians often represented as a bird), presenting the Wedjat-eye, which symbolized health, strength, power, and so on.
>
> The positions of the figures' arms had particular meaning to the Egyptians. In front of the god is a standard with two arms raised in the Egyptian gesture for worship. The bird has one arm extended holding the eye, the other raised in greeting.

"Well, there you go," April said. "It's a 'standard with two arms raised.'"

"You mean like a flagpole or something?"

"I guess."

"Weird." David thought about the strange figures. "I think we still have lots to learn before we get to Abraham's 'greater knowledge.'"

April nodded. "That's okay. I'm sure Abraham didn't get it all at once. And we won't either."

"Nope. But it gives us a chance to study together." He smiled. "I like that."

"Me too." She tilted her head. "Maybe we'll be learning together for eternity."

David took her hand. "That's nice to think about." But his mind was somewhere else. Already, he was thinking about his job, about everything he was going to accomplish tomorrow. He really did have important things to do—things he could really feel good about. And if he did well, there'd be other assignments too, possibly even more important than this one. He didn't know where all of this might lead, but he felt sure it would be someplace good.

CHAPTER 8

S miling with satisfaction, April leaned back in the dark leather chair. She did miss having David around. But, on the other hand, having some time to herself in the villa's beautiful library wasn't such a bad thing. Using the Internet on the library's computer, she'd been learning a lot about Egyptian history and religion, the pyramids, hieroglyphics, and much more. In fact, she was beginning to see some parallels between the ancient Egyptian religious beliefs and the temple, taking notes to share with David later. In particular, she was fascinated by what seemed to be some sort of sign language in the poses of people depicted in murals—all of those angular arms and outstretched hands. But what did it mean? There was more to it than met the eye—she felt sure of that.

She'd also learned more about Cairo itself—really just looking for things to do while David was at work. The city was much larger than she'd realized; altogether the metropolitan area had a population of nearly eighteen million people. And when Minkabh had said it was possible to find nearly any kind of activity, he hadn't been exaggerating. Besides the many museums, there were concerts, theaters, shopping malls, bazaars, restaurants, parks, a zoo, and even an aquarium—and, of course, the numerous archaeological sites. How could she possibly choose from this enormous wealth of activities? The answer was obvious: She should just ask Sharifa, Minkabh's wife. She would know all the good places to go—and which ones were within walking distance, too.

April descended the several flights of stairs down to the main living area, where Sharifa was sitting in a large easy chair, surrounded by colorful cushions. She was knitting some kind of yarn in variegated colors, using the biggest knitting needles April had ever seen.

"What are you making?" April asked.

"I thought I'd make a shawl for Kakra."

"How nice."

"Yes, I think she'll like it. Do you knit?"

April shook her head. "No. I'm not very talented, I'm afraid."

Sharifa looked up at her. "Nonsense. Everyone is talented in some way. And besides, you can start knitting just by following a pattern. And as you follow the pattern, the shawl magically appears." She widened her eyes dramatically. "Would you like to learn how?"

"Um, sure," April said. "But you'll have to show me what to do."

Sharifa spent the next half hour teaching April how to hold the needles, how to get started, the difference between "knit" and "purl," and much more. A half hour after that, April had a long, rather lumpy braid of red yarn curling onto the floor.

"This is fun," April said.

"I'm glad you like it." Sharifa replied. Then she leaned over and whispered conspiratorially, "It can be rather addicting."

April laughed.

A few moments later, Kakra wandered in from playing outside.

"Kakra!" Sharifa said. "Where's Nanny?"

"'Sleep in the garden."

Sharifa laughed. "The nanny is supposed to be watching her, but she's an older woman, and sometimes . . . well, you see."

Kakra sidled up to April, her brown eyes shining. "What are you making?"

April stared at her creation. "I have no idea. What do you think it is?"

Kakra thought for a moment. "I think it is a belt."

"Hmmm. I think you're right. Would you like to put it on?"

Kakra nodded, her finger in her mouth.

"All right. Here." April cut the yarn and tied it off. Then she wrapped the long, red "belt" around Kakra's waist and tied it in the front. "There! That looks very nice."

Kakra smiled brightly, her eyes sparkling with enjoyment.

"She's so beautiful!" April said, suddenly yearning for something she didn't quite understand.

"What do you say to April?" Sharifa asked.

"Thank you," Kakra replied shyly.

"That's right. That's the polite thing to do."

The little girl smiled, then coughed.

"What is that cough?" Sharifa asked. She put down her knitting and pulled the child over to her, looking intently into her face. "Your nose is running." She pulled a tissue from a box on the nearby table. "Here, blow." Kakra submitted reluctantly to the tissue. Then Sharifa put her hand on the girl's forehead. "Do you feel sick, my darling?"

Kakra shook her head.

"If you ever feel sick, you must tell Momma. All right?"

"Yes, Momma."

"Does she get sick a lot?" April asked.

Sharifa shook her head. "But her brother . . ." She couldn't finish.

"I'm sorry."

She cleared her throat. "Naturally, we worry now."

"Can you tell me what happened?"

Sharifa waved her hand. "Another time, perhaps."

"I understand." April held out her hands to the little girl. "Would you like to sit on my lap?"

Kakra nodded, and April lifted the child up onto her knees.

"You have a way with children," Sharifa said.

"Thanks. I have lots of nieces and nephews back in the U.S."

Sharifa nodded. "And how are you doing, now that David has gone back to work?"

"Fine, I guess. I miss him. But I'm finding things to do, and I'm glad he gets to come home at night. His boss said sometimes he can do his work on the computer here."

"That would be good." Sharifa continued knitting.

"He's trying really hard for a promotion."

Sharifa raised her eyebrows. "He is ambitious, then."

April frowned. "I wouldn't call it that. Now that we're married, he thinks it's important to get ahead."

"That is possible. But in my experience, men are complex creatures. They say they are working hard to provide for their family, but inside they also have a need to feel important, to be looked up to and admired by those around them."

April nodded. "I suppose we all do."

Sharifa sighed. "Yes. But I think the world would be better if we stopped trying to impress others and just took care of ourselves and our families. We should mind our own business."

April wasn't sure how to respond. Finally she said, "I think that's very wise."

Sharifa smiled and went on with her knitting.

"So where's Minkabh today?"

Sharifa shook her head. "You mean now? Who knows? He comes and goes as he pleases. This morning he was probably at the coffeehouse, talking with his friends and getting the latest news." She smiled. "Men say women are the ones who gossip, but I think it is otherwise."

"Maybe so."

"And are you going out today?" Sharifa looked up at April.

"Well, I really came down to ask you about places I could go—maybe places nearby."

"There's a wonderful bazaar just a few blocks down the street. You can easily walk there from here. But I must warn you"—she paused, narrowing her eyes—"you will see all kinds of things you will want to buy."

April laughed. "That sounds perfect."

"All right, then. You know . . ." Sharifa thought for a moment. "You should take a backpack in case you do find things you want to bring home. Then you could also take along a bottle of water and a snack or two."

"That would be great!"

Sharifa held up her finger. "Just a minute; I'll be right back." She put down her knitting, then disappeared into the hallway leading to the kitchen. A few minutes later she returned with a small black back-pack. A bottle of water was sticking out of one of the pockets. "Here you are," she said. "There is also an orange and a banana in the large pocket in case you get hungry."

"That's so nice of you! Thank you."

"It is my pleasure."

❧

The sunlight was glaring as April stepped out of the villa and onto the broad walkway leading to the street. She'd slung her backpack over her shoulders, but it didn't weigh much, and, in spite of the heat, it felt good to be outside and walking along in the fresh air. As she passed through the gates and onto the sidewalk, she was a little worried—everything seemed so foreign, so different, and this was her first time alone in the city.

She passed a group of soldiers who seemed to be just hanging around a government building, smoking cigarettes. But April could see they were watching the passersby carefully, their hands on their rifles. One thing she hadn't noticed before was the shabbiness of their uniforms. Most of the soldiers had patches on their knees and elbows, and April was surprised to see that their boots were coming apart, held together only by extra laces wrapped haphazardly around the leather.

Even the city itself looked different, now that she was on foot rather than riding in Minkabh's Mercedes. For the first time, instead of the modern office buildings, April noticed the decrepit shops tucked into the side streets, the crumbling mosques and ragged stalls. A donkey cart full of watermelons creaked wearily past. The very air seemed ancient, the sunlight full of dust. It was an *old* city.

As she passed a construction site on the other side of the street, she noticed the workers sitting on a plank at the top of the metal scaffolding and eating their lunch roughly twelve feet above the sidewalk. Without thinking, April waved, and to her embarrassment the men immediately began whistling and jeering. One of them, a bald fellow sporting a large, black mustache, called out in broken English, "Hey, bay-bee! You like nice Egyptian man?"

April just kept walking, looking straight ahead; she wouldn't make that mistake again. Everyone kept saying how safe the city was, but was it really? She was a long way from home, in a very strange place, and she found herself getting a little emotional. Forcing herself not to cry, she lifted her chin and walked on, a little faster than before. Somehow, she kept telling herself, everything would be all right. It had to. Didn't it?

CHAPTER 9

After spending several hours lounging with his friends at the coffeehouse, Minkabh had gone for a stroll through the marketplace, stopping long enough to buy a sandwich for lunch at one of the sidewalk food stands. Now he was sitting on a bench in a nearby park, enjoying the juicy treat and watching the pigeons scratching in the gravel lane that wound through the palm trees. He looked at his watch—1:07—wondering idly how someone so impatient could always manage to be so late. Finally, Runihura came into view, his hands stuffed into his pockets, his skinny arms tucked in at his sides. As he approached the bench, Minkabh looked at him steadily, his eyes narrowing. "You are late—again."

Runihura shrugged, then sat at the other end of the bench, looking at the ground. "What does it matter?"

"It matters to me."

"Why? You are the one who always says we must take things slowly—who is never ready to *act*." He looked at Minkabh sharply.

"And now *you* are ready to act?"

Runihura shook his head. "Not yet. But this week I will buy my last sacks of fertilizer. Saturday I will mix the fertilizer with rocks and fuel oil in the barrels. And Sunday, precisely at noon, I will drive the bus through the wall of the embassy."

"You are truly willing to die?"

"I will go to the gardens of paradise, and the Americans will find themselves in the fires of eternal torment."

Minkabh nodded. "You have warned the others?"

"Yes. Our allies will leave early for lunch that day."

"Then I am afraid you must *unwarn* them."

"What are you talking about?" Runihura leapt to his feet.

"You are premature."

"What! Why?"

"If you were ever on time to our meetings, you would know why. Not all of our agents have gotten through yet. There are still three who need visas."

"Always with you it is the same! Always we need more agents to get through! When will it be enough?"

Minkabh raised his chin. "It will be *enough* when we have the number specified in the plan we have all made together. And that is three more."

Runihura's lips tightened. "Then you had better get them through before Sunday at noon."

"I am afraid that will not be possible."

Runihura started to shake. "*Why* will it not be possible?"

"Because the American agent is in the way."

Runihura grabbed the front of Minkabh's shirt. "Then you will get him *out* of the way."

But Minkabh had had enough. He exploded with fury, pushing out with his big hands, sending Runihura flying backward onto the gravel path. "What do you think I have been *trying* to do, you *stupid* little man? Do you think I have been doing nothing? I am working with him; my wife is working with his wife. But if he does not respond, I will do whatever is necessary."

Runihura struggled to his feet, breathing hard, his hands trembling. "Fine. Just get him out of the way so the visas can be approved. But I warn you now—on the grave of my father I warn you—on Sunday at noon I will drive that bus through the embassy wall, regardless of what you think. So you had better send your little friend back home to America. Or kill him—it makes no difference to me. I am tired of waiting."

Minkabh rubbed his face, his eyes, feeling the weight of his responsibilities. He was tired himself—tired of working so hard, tired of having this same conversation over and over, tired of playing one side against the other. And perhaps he *had* moved too slowly, too cautiously; maybe Runihura was right. Maybe now was the time for action.

Finally, he nodded. "Very well. It will not be easy, but somehow I will get everything taken care of. And you will do what you are going to do." And with that, he felt a flood of relief. After all these years, it would finally be over. His revenge on the Americans would be complete.

Despite her frightening experience that morning, April discovered the bazaar to be quite an enjoyable place. All of the people seemed so nice, so hospitable to Americans. Of course, they *were* all trying to sell her something. But maybe things really would be all right. Already she'd found some beautiful yarn she could use in her knitting, and the textiles in the marketplace were amazing, a jumbled extravagance of textures and colors. Now, though, she was looking for something for David—something he might actually be able to use.

She stopped at a booth selling items crafted from wood and brass; a small wooden box had caught her eye. After nodding to the merchant, she picked up the box and opened it. It contained a compass, beautifully made, mounted on a brass swivel so the compass would always remain level. David would love it. He would put it on his desk as a reminder to stay on course.

Hmm, she thought, changing her mind. *I think he's focused enough already.* She put the compass back in its place on the merchant's blanket, then moved on to the next stall. There, to her surprise, the merchant had displayed a large cross on the back of his stand.

"Hello," April said. "You're a Christian?"

The man nodded. "It gives me much trouble. But my neighbors in the marketplace have learned to tolerate me." He leaned over and hollered to the man in the next stall: "Is that not true, Achmed?"

The man rolled his eyes, spat on the ground, and said dryly, "Oh, yes. I love you like a brother."

"You see?"

April laughed. "He doesn't sound very sincere."

The man smiled. "It is no matter." He gestured at the table in front of him. "Is there something here to your liking?"

"I'm looking for something for my husband."

"I have a beautiful watch here—a stunning Rolex knockoff."

April laughed again, then shook her head, looking over the merchandise. "That's a beautiful book, though." She picked up a small volume bound in red leather and decorated with gold leaf. The spine, too, was labeled in gold: "New Testament."

"For you," the man said, "ten American dollars."

April opened the backpack pocket where she'd put her wallet, then pulled out a ten-dollar bill.

The man shook his head. "You have much to learn, I'm afraid."

"What do you mean?"

"You should *never* pay what someone asks. Always counter with a lower offer."

April laughed. "Okay. But you shouldn't *tell* people that."

The man shrugged. "What can I do? We should treat others as we want to be treated—should we not?"

April nodded. "In that case, I insist you take the ten dollars."

"Well," the man said, "you have me there." He thought for a moment, then raised a finger. "But wait!" He rummaged around in a box under the table before bringing out the biggest multipurpose pocketknife April had ever seen. "It is the perfect gift for your husband." He began opening the blades. "See," he said, "it has a fine cutting blade. Also a fork and spoon. Two screwdrivers. A saw blade. And much more—look." He pulled a tiny metal flashlight from a slot on the top. "Also, on the side, a compass." He turned the knife over, revealing the tiny instrument embedded in the red plastic case. He slid the flashlight back into place and hefted the knife on his palm. "This knife alone is twenty dollars, but I will give you the knife and book *together* for twenty. What do you say?"

April paused. "Fifteen." She couldn't help but grin.

"Eighteen."

April raised an eyebrow. "Seventeen."

"Done!"

Later, her purchases stuffed into her backpack, April began to feel hungry. The smell of cooking food permeated the marketplace, and the lamb kebabs she kept seeing at some of the stalls looked particularly delicious. So she bought one, then sat on a bench under an olive tree, munching contentedly on the savory meat and vegetables.

After she finished, she pulled the banana out of a backpack pocket and ate that for dessert. Finally, keeping her arm over the backpack next to her, she closed her eyes to rest for a minute.

I should probably head for home, she thought. But she was just so *tired.*

She sat a few minutes more, then stood to leave. But suddenly, feeling queasy, she sat back down.

That's not good, she told herself. She thought about the lamb kebab. Hadn't Minkabh said that the food stands were safe? And then she knew she *had* to stand up, or things would go very badly.

She got off the bench and moved quickly behind the tree where no one would see her. Kneeling down, she threw up onto the dirt. Then again. And again. After resting a minute, she got to her feet, still a little shaky but actually feeling much better.

I won't do that again, she thought. *From now on, I'll do my eating at home.* Standing up straight, she began walking back to the villa, where dinner would be ready soon. But she no longer felt like eating.

CHAPTER 10

At the embassy that day, David spent the morning just watching people. Pam stayed by his side, pointing out some of the people she suspected were the worst offenders in letting problematic visa applications go through. David was surprised at the attitude of some of the workers, and he was especially surprised at the posters on the walls.

Later, as the two worked together in their cramped basement office, David said, "So they actually let people put up pro-Hamas propaganda?"

"I don't know that anyone *lets* them. The posters just go up when no one is looking."

"And no one dares to take them down? Who's in charge here?"

"The American ambassador, Nicholas Hodges."

"Why isn't he doing something?"

Pam smiled. "He is. He's the one who got the FBI involved. But he wants a careful investigation and a long-term solution—one that's more than just ripping posters off the wall."

"Yeah, well, that wouldn't be a bad place to start."

"They'd just go up again the next day."

David grunted. He was just opening his lunch sack to pull out an orange when his cell phone rang. It was Wilcox.

"Hi, boss. What's going on?"

"Interesting news. The president is coming to Cairo on Thursday."

"*The* president? As in president of the United States Alicia Morales?"

"That's right."

"Why?"

"For starters, her advisors think the attack on the ambassador's residence was just a warning—the embassy could very well be next."

"Attacking the embassy wouldn't be easy. The terrorists would have to get through the guardhouse barriers first. Someone on the inside would have to lower them."

"Exactly. So you need to make sure that doesn't happen. More work, I know, but there it is."

"What else?"

"She'll be meeting with the Egyptian authorities, of course, trying to get them to crack down before something big happens. And she's going to have a chat with the ambassador about security in general— and the problems at the embassy. Rumor is there may be a changing of the guard."

David whistled. "Anything else?"

"Just that you'll need to step it up. You know the terrorists will."

❧

As the afternoon dragged on, though, David didn't feel like "stepping it up." In fact, he felt like taking a nap. FBI agents on television were portrayed as glamorous and exciting, but in real life, the work often amounted to little more than sheer drudgery—collecting data, sifting through information, cutting through red tape.

David was just about to comment on the monotony when Pam stood up. "It's so hot in here!" she said. She stretched and took off her jacket, hanging it over the back of her chair. Then she casually opened the top two buttons of her white silk blouse.

Trying not to notice, David continued working on his computer. But then Pam knelt on her chair, bending across the desk over the yellow legal pads she'd arranged on the work surface so David could read them. She reached over and touched his arm. "Here," she said. "Look at this and tell me what you think."

But David was trying *not* to look—that was the problem. He fought to stay focused on the papers, but his eyes wanted to drift up to what his old seminary teacher had jokingly referred to as "low and behold." Was Pam doing this on purpose? He didn't know. But he did know he'd better be careful. He was just getting ready to take one of the legal pads and turn away when the phone rang.

David picked it up, grateful for the distraction, and cleared his throat. "Agent Hunter," he said.

"The very man I'm looking for." The voice on the phone was rough and low, almost a whisper.

"How can I help you?"

"You can help yourself—by getting out of Egypt. As I've told you before, your life is in danger. Do you not value your life?"

Putting his hand over the mouthpiece, David whispered to Pam, "Can we trace this?"

She shook her head, then whispered back, "No equipment."

David rolled his eyes, then went back to the phone. "Look, I have a job to do—and no one is going to scare me away."

"I'm not trying to scare you. I am your friend, even if you don't believe me."

David let out an exasperated sigh. "How do you know I'm in danger? And why should you care?"

"I know because I have friends in low places. I care because I have friends in high places."

"Who are you?"

"That does not matter. But believe me when I say that something big is coming soon—so big it will make your investigation meaningless, your life as a twig in the storm. You *must* leave Egypt—at once."

"Why should I trust you?"

"I have seen your beautiful wife. If I wanted to, I could have taken her already—to *make* you listen."

David felt the blood drain from his face. "Is that a threat?"

"Not at all. If I were your enemy, I would not hesitate. But you see, I have not touched her. Therefore, I am your friend. But you must leave *now.* Please, I beg you."

"When will—"

But the phone had gone dead. David slammed the receiver into its cradle.

"Who was that?" Pam asked.

"I don't know—someone who wants us to stop our investigation."

"What did he say?"

"He said our lives are in danger."

"Are they?"

David didn't know what to say. But he knew what he thought: If they weren't in danger, they soon would be. He shook his head. He couldn't think about that. He had a job to do.

In the back of the coffeehouse, the members of the council were speculating excitedly about the purpose of this emergency meeting.

Everyone had arrived on time—even Runihura—and now they were simply waiting for Baruti Massri, their white-haired leader, to begin the meeting. He came through the curtain, pulling it closed behind him. He raised his hand, signaling the group to be quiet.

"I have exciting news," he said. "Our sources have learned that the president of the United States is coming to Cairo on Thursday to meet with the American ambassador. I have called you here to discuss ways we might turn her visit to our advantage."

Runihura immediately spoke up. "What is there to discuss? We must move up the day of the bombing. What could be greater than to kill the president?"

"Could you be ready by then?"

The little man paused. "I will find a way."

"You seem unsure."

Minkabh stood up and looked around at the men of the council. "Yes," he said, "this is a marvelous opportunity. But should we really abandon our plans to take advantage of it? By next week, all of the visas will be approved, and we can finally take the destruction to American soil. If we kill the president now, our plans may never come to fruition. The American retribution will be swift—and terrible."

Runihura sprang to his feet. "As always, you lack the courage to do what must be done." He raised his skinny arm, pointing his bony finger at the big man. "You are no Egyptian; you are not even a man. You have no idea where your loyalties lie—and neither do we. Why don't you go join the Americans? You might as well be one of them."

In a flash, Minkabh crossed the room and smashed his big fist into Runihura's face. The little man fell to the floor, holding his nose with both hands, the blood streaming over his lips and onto his chin. Minkabh stepped back, shaking, while one of the other men helped Runihura to his feet and into a chair.

Minkabh looked around at the men, all of whom were staring at him with disgust. "I—I'm sorry," he said.

Baruti motioned for Minkabh to sit down, then raised his hand. "We will push through as many visas as we can," he said. "But we will move up the day of the bombing. It will take place Thursday rather than Sunday. Runihura will have the honor. Minkabh will see to the last of the visas."

❧

That night, David felt exhausted. In spite of his promise the night before, he'd worked longer than he should have, and he was still thinking about the disturbing phone call warning him to leave Egypt. The encounter with Pam hadn't helped, either—but he tried to put that out of his mind. He decided not to tell April about any of it.

"I need to turn in," he finally told her.

"Me too."

They climbed the stairs and got ready for bed.

"Did you have a nice day?" David asked.

"Yes—but I was hoping we could have more time together tonight."

"I'm sorry."

"You said you'd be home earlier. You *promised.*"

"I know."

"It's important to keep your promises, David. This isn't just something you can brush off. You have responsibilities."

"That's why I had to work so late. I—"

"Will you please forget about work for five minutes? I was talking about your responsibilities to *me.*"

David sighed. "I can't always be here whenever you need me. Sometimes I have to do what I have to do."

"I understand that. But you said you'd be home on time, and then you weren't. I was worried that something had happened to you."

"Okay, I get it. I'm sorry. But there are some scary people out there, and we need to stop them as soon as we can. Plus I found out today that the president is coming—she'll be here on Thursday."

"President Morales?"

"Yup."

"Wow. Will you get to meet her?"

"I don't know. But I do know her visit means more work. I'm sorry, but there's not much I can do about it."

April nodded. "I'll try to be patient. Just don't say one thing and then do something else. Okay?"

He picked up her hand and kissed it. "Okay. I'll do better. And I really will try to be here as much as I can. The rest of this week will be kind of hectic, but after that I'll make it up to you."

"Promise?"

David flushed. "Yes, I *promise*."

"Okay." She gave him a peck on the cheek. "I'll be counting on it."

"So what did you do today? I want to hear all about it."

"I had a really good time at the marketplace. *I* learned how to dicker." She smiled.

"Good for you! Find anything good?"

"Maybe." She fluttered her eyelashes.

"Ooh, what did you get me?"

She reached over and picked up her bulging backpack. She unzipped it and bright colors spilled out.

"Yarn? You got me yarn?"

April tried not to laugh. "You know," she said, "you're only about half as funny as you think you are."

"Oh, really? Then why are you smiling?"

April tried to sound serious. "If you must know, the yarn is for me; Sharifa is teaching me how to knit."

"That's nice."

April nodded. "It's fun." She removed the packages of yarn and pulled out the knife. "Here's what I got for you."

"Wow!" David said. Then he started to laugh. "This is the biggest Swiss army knife I've ever seen."

April frowned. "You don't like it?"

"No, no—I love it! It's great!" He unfolded the spoon. "I can eat breakfast with it."

"You don't like it—I can tell."

He laughed. "Yes I do. But I can't exactly carry it around in my pocket. It's too big."

"Do you think so? I was trying to get something you could use."

"I can use it. I can take it camping and stuff." Then he thought of something. "I can't take it home on the plane, though. No way this will make it through security."

She shook her head. "Oh no, I didn't think about that."

"It's okay. I think we can put it in our luggage."

"What if someone opens our luggage and steals it?"

"Don't be silly; nobody will steal it." But David could tell she was getting emotional. He took her hand and pulled her close to him. "Are you okay?"

She shook her head. "I don't know. You're gone so much—and I think I'm homesick." She choked back a sob.

Smiling, he took her into his arms. "It'll be okay. We should be able to go home in a week or so."

"I'm ready now."

"I know."

She pulled back, then wiped her eyes. "I'll be all right." She sniffed.

"Are you sure?"

She nodded. "Here, I'll show you what else I bought." She opened the backpack to get her New Testament, but there, along with it, was a folded sheet of paper. She pulled it out.

"What's that?" David asked.

"I don't know. I didn't put it in there. Maybe somebody slipped it in the backpack while I was at the marketplace." She unfolded the paper and read it aloud. "'I have warned your husband. Now I am warning you. You must leave Egypt immediately. Your lives are in danger. I am your friend.'" For a moment she didn't say anything. Finally, she blurted out, "David, what is this? Has someone warned you about this?"

David didn't know what to say. "I . . . well . . . Yes. But I didn't think I should tell you; I didn't want you to worry. And I have a job to do. I can't back down at every threat. This kind of thing comes with the territory; I thought you understood that. Maybe this is somebody's way of getting rid of us, of stopping my investigation."

April shook her head. "I don't care. I think we should leave. I think we should go back home." She raised her eyes, the tears running down her cheeks. "What if you get killed?"

"I'm not going to get killed. And besides, it's like you've always said—*somebody* has to do this job. In the past, you've always encouraged me."

"I know. But things are different now."

"Why? What's different?"

She paused. "I think I might be pregnant."

"Really?"

She nodded.

"How can you be pregnant? I thought . . ."

"I know."

David shook his head. "You're not pregnant; you wouldn't be having symptoms this early. Would you?"

"It's possible."

"I don't think so. You're just tired—we both are. It's been a long day. Let's go to bed. Things will look better in the morning."

April sighed, wiping her eyes. "Maybe you're right."

David kissed her softly.

"But please," April said, "be careful. I'd hate to lose you."

"Don't worry," he said. "Nothing bad is going to happen."

CHAPTER 11

The next morning, April actually did feel better. After David had gone to work, she spent some time knitting and then learning more about ancient Egypt. But after a while, she needed to get out of the house. She took a brief walk, then decided to go see David. *I'll just brighten up his day a little,* she thought with a smile. She moved briskly along, wondering what David's office—and his partner—looked like. When she reached the embassy, she pushed through the big glass doors and approached the receptionist's desk, where a woman was answering phones. The woman looked up. "May I help you?"

"I'd like to see David Hunter, please."

The woman checked April's papers, then looked at a directory on her desk. "Take the elevator to the basement. Second door on the left."

"Thanks," April said.

It's not much to look at, April thought, noticing the rough concrete walls, the plain wooden doors. She pushed open the second door.

90

There was David, sitting across the desk from his partner, both typing away on their computers.

"Hi," April said. "Surprise!"

"April! What are you doing here?"

"I thought you might like to get some lunch." She looked over at his partner.

David stood up. "Oh, April, this is my partner, Pam. Pam, meet my wife, April."

"Hi," Pam said, flashing a smile. "Nice to meet you."

"You too," April said. The woman *was* beautiful—even though David had tried to play that down. April had hoped she'd be a little plainer—and a little older. And she thought Pam was smiling maybe just a little *too* much.

April turned back to David. "So what do you think? Hungry?"

"Actually, yes. But I've got to finish this while I have my mind around it. If I don't, it will take me forever to figure it out again. Complicated stuff. Sorry. Maybe tomorrow?"

"Okay. But then it won't be a surprise."

"Another day, then."

"Another day when you're too busy?"

"I . . . uh . . ."

"It's okay," April said. "We can go tomorrow."

"Great," David said. "It's a date."

⌘

April was lying on the bed looking up at the ceiling. *I should have called first,* she thought. *I put David in an awkward position.* And, she realized, she'd been a little snotty with her comment about how he was too busy for her. She felt the guilt creeping up in her chest. *Okay, okay,* she thought, rolling her eyes. *I'll call and apologize.* She sat up, picked up the phone, and dialed David's number. But David didn't answer; instead, a receptionist came on the line. "American embassy. How may I help you?"

"David Hunter's office, please."

"I'm sorry. He and his partner have gone to lunch."

"Thanks," April said. "Thanks a lot." She slammed down the phone. Then she rolled over on the bed, putting her face into her pillow.

⁜

That night, April was unusually quiet. David tried to joke with her, but she was having nothing to do with it. Finally he gave up and watched television in silence. April watched for a little while, but finally she went upstairs—much earlier than usual—without saying a word. A few minutes later, David followed her. To his surprise, their bedroom door was closed.

Turning the knob, he went in. "Did you have a nice day?" he asked.

April was getting ready for bed. "Not really."

David didn't know what to say. "Are you mad at me or something?"

April didn't answer.

"April, I've never seen you like this. What in the world is going on?"

Finally, she looked over at him. "That's exactly what I want to know."

"What do you mean?"

She held her chin up defiantly, her eyes shining. "You wouldn't go to lunch with me today. You didn't have time."

"I know; I was busy. I thought you understood that."

"I called later to see how you were doing. The receptionist said you and *Pam* had gone to lunch."

David's face fell. "*After* we got the work done."

"You couldn't take half an hour to go with me?"

"No. I told you. We had to finish what we were doing."

"Why didn't you call me later, after you finished? We could have gone to lunch then. I would have waited for you."

David shook his head. "I . . . I guess I could have."

"You didn't do it because you didn't want to. You wanted to go with Pam."

"April, that's not true."

"I saw how she was looking at you. She *likes* you. And you like her. You're *attracted* to her. Aren't you?" April's face was red, and she was breathing hard.

"April, look—"

"No, David, you look: If you don't want to be with me, you don't have to. You can sleep by yourself—on the couch in the library. I'm going to bed. Alone."

"April—"

She pushed him out of the bedroom, slamming the door behind him. He put his hand on the door, listening to her sobs. He knocked quietly. "April, let me in."

"Not tonight. I'm mad and I don't feel good. We can talk tomorrow."

"Okay." He paused. "I love you."

But April didn't say anything. He waited for a moment, wondering whether to say anything else, but then he thought better of it. He trudged down the hallway and tried to get comfortable in the library. The couch really wasn't so bad. But still, he knew, it would be a long time until morning.

❧

David lay on his back, staring at the ceiling. Then he rolled onto his side, closed his eyes, and waited. But it was no use; he couldn't stop *thinking*, let alone go to sleep. With a sigh, he sat up and turned on the light next to the couch. Deciding that he might as well do something useful, he went to the computer and fired up the Internet. Time to do some research; maybe it would get his mind off the fight with April.

He searched on the words "translate," "book," and "Abraham," and found himself rewarded with nearly two million hits. Ignoring the usual anti-Mormon propaganda, he clicked a link for "Book of Abraham" at Wikipedia. He found some interesting things there—most notably a reference to "The Egyptian Alphabet and Grammar," which he'd never heard of before but appeared to be some sort of analysis of characters from the book of Abraham papyrus—right up his alley. He smiled and cracked his knuckles, then typed some more. Further searching turned up actual photographs of some of the papyri Joseph Smith had owned.

As David looked through the characters on the papyri, he noticed a few that looked awfully familiar. Pulling out his wallet, he withdrew the transcript of characters from the Book of Mormon that he kept with him to remind him of his grandfather.

Sure enough, some of the characters were similar, and a few were obviously the same. That made sense to David since he knew the Book of Mormon was written in a form of Egyptian. But would the meaning be the same in this different context, from a different time and culture?

Jumping from link to link, David found excerpts from a book called *Symbol and Magic in Egyptian Art*, which noted that Egyptian signs and symbols were meant to be interpreted on many levels. Then he came across a similar passage in a talk given by Hugh Nibley, an LDS scholar he greatly admired: "You very often have texts of double meaning," Dr.

Nibley had said. "It's quite possible, say, that this 'Sensen' papyrus, telling a straightforward, innocent little story, should contain also a totally different text concealed within it. The Egyptians knew what they were doing, but we don't. We don't have the key."

The key, David thought. *What could be the key?* In his work with codes and ciphers, David had used many keys to unravel secret messages. But this had to be different. Didn't it? Could the characters be read on some other level, in some other way? They were, after all, *hieroglyphics*—priestly writing. Maybe the priests had a way of hiding secrets that could be understood only by the initiated.

He thought about other languages with which he was familiar. Japanese characters were often composed of earlier Chinese symbols that carried their own independent meanings—something he found quite fascinating. He thought of the character for "forest," which was simply three "tree" symbols combined into one, and of the character for the Japanese game of *go,* which combined, one on top of the other, the Chinese symbols for "slate" and "shell"—the materials of which the playing pieces were made.

碁

Could some of the Egyptian characters follow a similar system? And if so, what would it be? And then David remembered: Minkabh had said that the book of Abraham was a Jewish book! Could ancient Hebrew actually be *older* than Egyptian? Quickly he went to the language section of the library and scanned the titles. Minkabh had a lot of books, but David quickly found what he was looking for: a dictionary of Hebrew words. The book included an introduction to the Hebrew alphabet, and seeing it made him think of Joseph Smith and the other early Brethren studying Hebrew at Kirtland. The thought made him smile.

As he browsed through the characters and their pronunciations, his FBI training kicked into gear, and he began linking the characters mentally with what he'd seen on the papyri. Could there be a connection? Taking the book back to the computer, he picked out a character from the papyrus—obviously a shorthand image of an enthroned god—and transcribed it onto some paper:

Then he scanned the Hebrew characters, looking for similarities, searching for anything that might be combined to create the Egyptian hieroglyphic. It wasn't long until he found some. There was *Kof,* the shepherd's crook:

And there was *Lamed,* the flail, or whip:

And finally, he noted *Beth,* meaning house:

He had to turn the characters in various ways, but together they could definitely be put together to form the Egyptian character he'd drawn on the paper:

"Thy rod and thy staff they comfort me," David thought. The staff was the shepherd's crook, used to rescue the wandering sheep. The flail was the rod, used to fight off predators. *Mercy and justice—the essential attributes of the Great God, linked as one in God's house.*

And then David noticed: Reading the combined characters from top to bottom, they were *Kof, Lamed, Beth,* with the sounds *K, L, B,* or, as a Hebrew might say them together, *Kolob.* It was the dwelling place of God, with the very name used in the book of Abraham. David jumped up with excitement. Could this be the key? Could it really be that simple? He didn't know. But he could hardly wait to tell April about his discovery—if he could just get her to talk to him.

CHAPTER 12

April slept late the next morning. She heard David knocking on her door before going to work, but she decided not to answer. She felt better than she had the night before, but she was still mad. She decided she was going to do something she'd been wanting to do since their excursion last Saturday. And she wasn't going to tell David.

After getting dressed in jeans and a T-shirt, she gathered her things and picked up David's knife—something he obviously didn't want—and threw everything into her backpack. Then, with the backpack on her shoulder, she went downstairs, out the back door of the villa, and down the winding stone path that led to the carriage house, where Donkor, Minkabh's driver, lived with his wife. Timidly, she knocked, and Donkor opened the door.

"Well, good morning, Mrs. Hunter."

"Good morning. Would you have time to take me somewhere?"

"Of course. Where would you like to go?"

"The Necropolis."

He raised his eyebrows. "That terrible place? Why would you want to go there?"

"I feel sorry for those people. I want to take them some food."

"That's kind of you." He smiled. "But there are six million of them. What can any one person do?"

"I can help a few of them."

Donkor nodded. "That's true. Very well. Give me a few minutes to get ready, and we'll be on our way."

Donkor took April to the marketplace, where she bought six large bags of bread, fruit, and vegetables. Then they drove to the edge of the city and out into the tombs. April kept looking out the window, watching for the boys she'd seen earlier, but they were nowhere in sight. Instead, she noticed a woman and her three young children cooking something over a fire. "Please," she said, "pull over here."

The car stopped, and April got out, lifting one of the heavy bags. "Here," Donkor said. "I will help you." He came around and took all of the bags, then walked with April toward the woman and her family.

"Hello," April said. The woman stood up. Her face was dirty, and her clothes were little better than rags. April knew that life in the Necropolis was hard, but she was still surprised at the woman's condition. Trying to ignore the smell, April put out her hand. "My name is April."

"I am Eshe." She ducked her head, then timidly took April's hand and smiled.

April smiled back. The children gathered around her, reaching up to touch April's long blonde hair, her pale white skin.

"They have not been so close to an American before," Eshe explained haltingly.

"It's all right." April looked down at the children, then down at the fire, where two small animals were roasting. At first she couldn't tell what they were—the skin had reddened and the hair was scorched off. Then she realized—the family was cooking rats. For a moment she was afraid she was going to throw up. But she looked away from the fire, trying to concentrate on the woman and her children. "I've brought food," she managed to say.

The woman looked puzzled. "Food? For us?"

"Yes." She motioned for Donkor to hand the woman one of the bags.

"Why?"

"So you'll have something good to eat."

Tears came to the woman's eyes. "Why us?"

"Why not you?"

The woman shrugged. "There are so many here."

April nodded. "I know. Will you give the rest of this food to other families?"

"Yes, of course. Thank you."

"I'm glad to help. I'll bring more tomorrow."

"You will bring more?" The woman's eyes widened in disbelief.

"Please, just share the food with others. I'll come again."

The woman nodded but didn't say anything else. She was still staring as April and Donkor pulled away in the large, black Mercedes, a shining chariot from another world.

❧

David dialed the phone number, then waited as the phone rang on the other end of the line.

"Hello?" Sharifa answered. David could hear Kakra playing in the background.

"Hello, this is David. Is April there?"

"I'm sorry, David. She is still out."

"Do you know where she went?"

"No, I'm afraid not."

"All right." David sighed. "When she gets back would you ask her to call me?"

"Yes, I will."

"Thank you."

David hung up the phone, then leaned back in his chair, staring up at the ceiling in the basement office at the embassy. He just hated this. He'd called several times earlier, with the same result, and now he was getting worried—finding it almost impossible to work.

"Still not there?" Pam asked.

David shook his head.

"She must really be mad at you."

"I'm afraid so."

She reached over and touched his arm. "She'll be okay."

"I know." He rubbed his eyes and stretched. "But never mind. We've got work to do."

They spent the next few hours entering their notes into the computer, with David reading aloud from the yellow pads and Pam typing on the keyboard. Occasionally they'd stop to discuss an event they'd recorded. Finally, David had had enough. "Let's take a break," he said.

"Good idea."

They walked upstairs to the vending machine and bought some drinks. David looked at his watch. "It's way past quitting time."

"I know. But we've got a lot more to do. We should really keep on working."

David shook his head. "I need to get home and find out what's going on with April."

Pam tilted her head. "You know," she said, "that's probably exactly what she wants. You watch—she won't be there. And you'll be even more worried until she finally comes home. And then you'll fawn all over her and tell her you're sorry. You don't realize it now, but that will set the pattern for the rest of your married life. Is that really what you want?"

David found the idea surprising, even insightful. "I'd never thought about it like that."

Pam grimaced. "Trust me. I know what I'm talking about."

"You've been married?"

She nodded. "About a year ago—to another agent. We were happy for a while, but we were both pretty competitive, always trying to get ahead. Eventually we were working so much, we hardly saw each other. I was working all the time, and I *thought* he was. Really, he'd been getting cozy with a woman who wasn't quite so aggressive—his partner, actually."

"I'm sorry."

She closed her eyes, accentuating the sensuousness in her face. "I guess I'm still mad about it. Even now, I keep thinking of ways to get back at him for leaving me. He was such a patriot—so loyal to his country. He just couldn't be loyal to me."

"You'll have to find a way to let that go. If you don't, it will get in the way of your work."

"I know. But I was crazy about him. And there are so many things I miss about being in a relationship." She smiled softly, sending a chill up David's spine. "What do you want to do?"

"Let's go back to the office. I'll call one more time. If April's not there, we'll work another hour or so." But David was getting a funny feeling in his stomach. Something wasn't right. But he wasn't sure what he was supposed to do about it.

❧

Back in the office, David dialed, then waited for someone to pick up the phone.

"Hello." But this time it was Minkabh rather than Sharifa.

"Hi, Minkabh. Is April there?"

"No, I'm sorry. She and Sharifa have gone to the movies."

"Oh, okay." He shook his head. "When she gets home, will you tell her I'm still working? I'll probably be pretty late getting home."

"All right, I'll tell her."

"Thanks."

He hung up the phone and picked up a yellow pad, ready to resume their work, but suddenly Pam was standing by his side.

"You know, David, you look exhausted."

"I'm okay. We should get back to work."

She nodded. "We will. But let me just rub your shoulders a few minutes. It will help a lot."

"I don't think that's such a good idea," David said. But already her hands were on his shoulders; already she was beginning to rub, slowly and softly.

"You're so tense. Just relax and let me make you feel better."

He could hear the softness of her breath, smell the sweetness of her perfume. Alarmed, David shrugged away from her touch.

Pam pulled back. "Is something wrong?"

"What are you trying to do?"

"I just—"

The phone rang. David leaned over and picked up the receiver. "Agent Hunter."

"David, this is Minkabh."

"Minkabh. Is everything all right?"

"Yes, as far as I know. But I was thinking—since our wives have gone to the movies, maybe you'd like to do something. We could have a 'boys' night out,' as you say in America. Are you sure your work can't wait until tomorrow?"

David breathed a sigh of relief. "Actually, that sounds great. What did you have in mind?"

"Well, it's a little unusual, but I found something new today at the tomb complex—another connection with Father Abraham. I thought you might like to see it."

"I would."

"I can be at the embassy in just a couple of minutes."

"Okay. I'll be ready." He turned to Pam. "Sorry, but Minkabh wants me to go with him someplace."

"You'd rather do that than work?" She smiled.

"We weren't really getting much done, were we."

"Oh, I wouldn't say that. I was hoping we could do a lot of things."

"You're a very scary lady, you know that?"

She shook her head. "I didn't mean—"

"Yes, you did. You knew exactly what you were doing."

Pam blushed. "You're an attractive man—so tall, with those big, brown eyes. It's not my fault you're so good-looking."

"You know I'm married."

Pam looked puzzled. "I didn't think men cared about that."

"*I* care," David said. And then it struck him how true that was. He *did* care. And he was going to do everything in his power to make things right with April.

CHAPTER 13

A few minutes later, the big Mercedes pulled up in front of the embassy, but Minkabh was driving. David got into the passenger seat. "Where's Donkor?"

"Driving our wives—in the Cadillac. And besides, we don't need him tonight."

David noticed a strange smell; the car's interior had a sharp, metallic scent. Had Minkabh been drinking? He turned to face the man. "I don't mean to offend you, but I thought Muslims didn't drink."

Minkabh smiled. "Are there no Mormons who drink?"

David nodded. "Okay, good point."

"Those who are truly devout do not drink—but sometimes I am not so devout." Minkabh pulled out a CD. "Music?"

"Sure," David said, trying to ignore the smell of alcohol. "What have you got?"

"American artist Lee Roy Parnell."

David started to laugh. "You listen to *country?*"

Minkabh shrugged. "What can I say? Good stuff."

He popped the disc into the player, then turned up the volume, singing badly off-key in his Egyptian accent. *"Don't underestimate the power of love,"* he bellowed along with the music. *"You're never down so low that it can't lift you up."*

David tried to keep a straight face but finally burst out laughing. "You're a terrible singer."

Minkabh smiled. "It is no matter."

"You're trying to make me feel better, aren't you."

"Perhaps."

"Well, it's working."

Minkabh nodded. "By the way, I have finished your book of Abraham." He picked up the triple combination from the leather seat and handed it to David.

"What do you think?"

"Many interesting things. I will show you more parallels tonight."

They drove for a few more minutes, out past the Necropolis and then up to the fence enclosing the ancient tomb complex. Minkabh got out and unlocked the gate, and then both men entered the enclosure, locking the gate behind them. Soon they were inside the tombs, shining their flashlights into the recesses along the halls and passageways.

"Do you remember where we were before?" Minkabh asked.

"Yes. But I wouldn't be able to find it on my own."

"That's all right; just follow me."

Minkabh led David through several narrow passages and shadowy doorways. He paused, then pushed against a large stone slab, which swung slowly open into the dark chamber. Golden artifacts glinted in the darkness. "Now do you know where we are?"

"Yes. How could I forget?"

"Could you find your way out if you had to?" Minkabh smiled, his large, white teeth gleaming in the darkness.

"I doubt it. It's easy to get turned around down here."

Minkabh wagged his index finger. "You should pay better attention. Sometime you might not have me with you to guide you."

David couldn't quite grasp what Minkabh was saying. "What do you mean?"

"I mean—" Minkabh began. Suddenly he grabbed David, forcing his hands up behind his shoulders. David knew how to fight, but the pain was excruciating, and the big man's strength was incredible. David pushed back as hard as he could, but it was like trying to budge an ox.

A few seconds later, it didn't matter anymore. Minkabh had fastened David's wrists and ankles with white plastic cable ties. Then he picked him up, carrying him like a child, and placed him carefully on top of the lion-couch altar, where he finished the job by fastening David's limbs to the altar with nylon rope. David tried to struggle, but the effort was useless.

"I thought this would be a fitting place," Minkabh said. He reached into his pocket and pulled out a large clasp knife, flicking open the shining steel blade, which locked into place with a click.

David didn't understand what was happening, but never before had he felt such terror. "What are you doing?" he managed to choke out.

"I have tried so hard to persuade you to leave Egypt. But you are a stubborn one, David Hunter."

David closed his eyes. "So it was you," he breathed.

Minkabh nodded. "We had three more visas to push through at the embassy. We tried and tried to do it, but you were always looking, always watching—even though your partner kept trying to distract you."

David looked up with a start. "You mean Pam is—"

Minkabh laughed. "One of us? Oh, yes. Frankly, I'm surprised you didn't know." He took a deep breath. "The plan was to get the visas approved by Sunday. Then, precisely at noon, an associate was to drive a bus loaded with explosives into the first floor of the embassy."

"And now?"

"With your president coming, our plans have changed. The bombing will still take place—but tomorrow rather than Sunday. So we are out of time. Hopefully with you out of the way, the visas can be pushed through in the morning."

"And then you'll kill the president."

Minkabh nodded.

"You'll have to get past the guardhouse first. There are barriers—"

Minkabh laughed. "We bribed the guards to leave for lunch a few minutes early. In their absence, Pam will lower the barriers."

"Pam? You're kidding. You'd trust her to do that?"

"Nekhbet will be standing by to make sure she does as she is ordered. Once Pam does this, you see, there will be no going back for her. Her loyalty will be secure. Then she will be of much use to us."

David groaned. "Why have you joined these men? You've helped the FBI for years. What happened?"

Minkabh grimaced. "Two years ago, my son, Kafele, fell sick—a rare form of cancer. Doctors here offered no hope, so we turned to our friends in America. They promised to help—'Certainly, certainly, anything for you, Minkabh'—but they did nothing more than place a few phone calls. I was angry, disappointed—disgusted. Finally, I contacted the doctors myself, the specialists in that field. But their schedules were full for many weeks, and they would not let other children die just to save mine. In the end, none of it made any difference; my son was dead."

David shook his head. "I'm sorry."

"I swore I would have vengeance. I would use my relationship with the Americans to destroy the Americans."

"And Pam?"

Minkabh shrugged. "Money."

"There's always something deeper than money."

"Well, there was her husband, of course. You've probably heard the story."

David nodded.

"It left her bitter, disillusioned—and easy to recruit."

"And you have to kill me?"

Minkabh sighed. "What else am I supposed to do with you? Tell me—if I let you go, what will you do?"

"Everything I can to stop you."

"So there it is; I have no choice. April, on the other hand, will be sent back to America. She will believe that you were killed in the line of duty, in the explosion at the embassy." Minkabh paused. "But I have a problem."

"What kind of problem?"

"My instructions are to kill you. But, I am sorry to say, I have come to think of you as a friend. And so, I now realize, I cannot follow through." He closed the knife and placed it back in his pocket.

David closed his eyes, sighing with relief.

"But neither can I let you go."

Suddenly, the fear was back. "What are you going to do?"

Minkabh shook his head. "I will leave you here, in the tombs. It would be more merciful for me to kill you, but I cannot do it. I'm sorry." He paused. "I will leave your flashlight on so you can see until it runs out of power. But after that you will be in darkness. And after a few days you will die, here in this resting place of the dead."

PART 3

CHAPTER 14

"And [God] said unto [Abram], I am the Lord that brought thee out of Ur of the Chaldees, to give thee this land to inherit it.

And [Abram] said, Lord God, whereby shall I know that I shall inherit it? And [God] said unto him, Take me an heifer of three years old, and a she goat of three years old, and a ram of three years old. . . . And [Abram] took unto him all these, and [cut] them in [half], and laid each piece one against another: . . . And when the sun was going down, a deep sleep fell upon Abram; and, lo, an horror of great darkness fell upon him. . . . And it came to pass, that, when the sun went down, and it was dark, behold a smoking furnace, and a burning lamp that passed between those pieces. [In this way] the Lord made a covenant with Abram."—Genesis 15:7–18

David could tell that the light from the flashlight was growing dimmer; even though his eyes had long ago become accustomed to the relative darkness, he could no longer see some of the details inscribed on the walls of the tomb. The shadows had grown deeper—the blacks blacker, the grays grayer—as if, second by second, his eyes themselves were failing. He'd already been praying a long time, but now he redoubled his efforts, begging for his life to be spared—for April's sake, and, if she really was pregnant, for the sake of their child. But Minkabh's son had not been spared, and surely Minkabh had prayed as sincerely, as feelingly, as David was now. Why should David expect special privileges when so much of the world was faced with untold terrors of suffering and death? He couldn't answer that question. All he knew was that he would continue to pray.

After a while, though, David's prayers turned into a kind of thinking, a series of questions about things he'd done. He thought about his argument with April. If he'd put her first, he realized, there wouldn't have been a fight. And he might not have been tempted to work so late. And he wouldn't have had the encounter with Pam. But what if Minkabh hadn't called? *Then I wouldn't be here now,* he thought, appreciating the irony.

Deep inside, David knew he wouldn't have given in to Pam—he loved April far too much for that. And, of course, there was the simple fact that it was wrong. But Pam's attempt at a "massage" had left him a bit shaken.

Maybe, he thought, *in some strange way, the Lord brought me here to get me out of there.* It was a startling idea, but it seemed to ring true. And if it really was true, then this could not be the end for him. With that thought, his smoldering faith sparked into flame. Somehow, he knew, the Lord would get him out of this mess too.

After getting home from the movies, April decided to go to bed early, but she couldn't keep from thinking about her fight with David the night before, and the more she thought about him working late with Pam—especially after their fight—the more worried she got. She tried to keep her mind from going down such troubling roads, but she couldn't seem to shake the idea. And she certainly wasn't getting any sleep. She looked over at the clock on the nightstand—nearly eleven o'clock. Shouldn't David be home by now? Finally, she decided she would wait up for him. She was feeling a lot better tonight, and maybe when he got back, they could have a more reasonable discussion about things—talking together, making their small jokes, apologizing. She could almost taste the sweetness of it.

After a while, she reached over and turned on the lamp by the bed, thinking maybe she'd read. But the words seemed meaningless, and she kept finding herself having to go back over paragraphs she'd just finished but hadn't even noticed. She simply couldn't help thinking about David—wondering if things were all right with him.

Eventually, she put down her book, slid out of bed, and got to her knees, praying that everything would be okay, that David would be safe, that they'd be able to resolve their differences. She wanted to feel the Lord's comfort, his reassuring touch, but as she continued to pray, she actually felt worse rather than better, became more worried rather than less. Something whispered that Pam was the least of David's problems, that he was facing dangers far more serious than April had imagined. And in her mind, she seemed to see David's face, his eyes closed, in a place with little light and many shadows.

Alarmed, she picked up the telephone from the nightstand and dialed David's office. The phone rang several times, but there was no answer. Could she have called the wrong number? She tried again, more carefully this time, but with the same result. David wasn't there. She tried his cell phone, which he always picked up, again with no answer.

Something was wrong, she could feel it. She could no longer just sit there; she had to *do* something. So she got dressed and picked up her backpack, then made her way down the flights of stairs to the living area. Everything was dark; everyone must have already gone to bed.

She went to the kitchen, opened the refrigerator, and threw some oranges and bananas into her backpack, along with four bottles of water and some granola bars. And then she realized she had no idea what she was doing or where she was going. All she knew was that she was going out to look for David—in a city of more than eighteen million people.

Sure, she thought, *that makes perfect sense.*

She knelt by the table and prayed again, asking for guidance, and as she pleaded, she remembered what she'd told David so long ago: "You can't always know things ahead of time. Sometimes you just have to go forward with faith." Now it was her turn to see how deeply she believed those words.

Quietly she went out the back door and over the path to the carriage house, wondering if Donkor had gone to bed. As she approached, she could see the orange tip of his cigarette glowing in the darkness, his shadowy form leaning back in a lawn chair near his front door.

"Mrs. Hunter!" he said, standing up. "What brings you out so late?"

"I'm worried about David. Do you know where he is?"

"He went with Minkabh to the tombs."

"This late?"

"They went some time ago, while we were at the movies. He left word with my wife." Donkor dropped his cigarette onto the pavement and ground it out with his heel. "I'm sorry I didn't tell you."

April felt relief wash over her, followed by another wave of worry; something still wasn't right. "Would you take me there?"

"To the tombs? Now?"

"Yes. Maybe we could meet them."

"Unless they're already on their way back. You might want to wait a bit more."

April shook her head. "I'd at least like to try."

Donkor nodded. "All right," he said. But he didn't look happy about it.

～

The tombs were only a few miles to the east, but in the darkness, the trip seemed to take forever, the lights of the city receding behind them and the shadows of the Necropolis rising to meet them. To April's surprise, electric lights cast a dull illumination here and there, even in the City of the Dead.

"They have electricity here?" she asked.

"Yes. It is provided by the city of Cairo."

"Even though it's illegal to live here?"

Donkor nodded.

A few minutes later, they were at the ancient tomb complex, just east of the Necropolis. And to April's relief, the big black Mercedes was parked outside the gate. "They're here!" she said. "Please, stop the car."

Donkor pulled up to the gate, and April opened the door. "Thanks, Donkor," she said. "I really appreciate it."

Donkor looked puzzled. "You're staying here?"

"Yes. I can ride home with David. I'll be fine."

"But to leave you alone—I'm not sure that's a good idea."

"Who else would be out here?"

Donkor paused, then looked at her solemnly. "Mrs. Hunter, this place is cursed. It is not a place for the living."

"Thank you, Donkor." She smiled. "But I don't believe in ghosts."

Donkor nodded. "Perhaps so. But please, be careful. Get in the Mercedes and lock the door. Do you have a flashlight?"

"No."

"Here, take mine." He fumbled around in the car's glove

compartment and pulled out a dusty, plastic flashlight that looked none too dependable.

"All right," she said. "Thanks."

Donkor nodded. "They shouldn't be much longer, I wouldn't think."

"Okay."

He waved as he pulled away, leaving April alone in the desert darkness.

With no desire to turn on the flashlight, she leaned against the trunk of the Mercedes, looking up at the stars. This far from the city, they were impressive indeed, the Milky Way swirling in glory across the blackness of space. And the night was so quiet! April closed her eyes. As she listened, she thought she could hear someone moving nearby. She pushed the switch on her flashlight, but nothing happened; it was dead.

And that's when she saw the ghost.

CHAPTER 15

"So Abraham cleaved to faith when he went down to Egypt.
. . . This can be compared to a person who was about to
descend into a deep pit and was afraid he would not be able
to come back up. What did this person do? He tied a length
of rope above the pit, saying 'Since I have tied this knot,
now I can enter.' Similarly, when Abraham was about to go
down to Egypt, he first tied a knot of faith, so he would
have something to grasp; then he descended."—The Zohar,
Vaera, 25:357

In the starlight, April could make out a figure crouching not far
from the gate. It was nearly invisible, but it was definitely there.
With fear rising in her throat, she tried to speak, but nothing
would come out. Finally, she managed to whisper, "Who's there?"

The figure didn't respond, but she thought she saw it move again.
Then she heard a voice, not from the figure but from inside the gate.
It was Minkabh, stumbling along with his flashlight. She watched to
see if David would appear, but Minkabh seemed to be alone. April was

about to call to him, to ask him about David, when he pulled a flask from his pocket and held it in the air.

"To David," he said. "To David . . . in the dark. May his sufferings be short." He took a long drink, smacking his lips.

April shrank back into the shadows. Now she knew what was wrong: Minkabh had left David in the tombs. But why?

And then, in a flash, she understood: Minkabh and Sharifa were the ones who had tried to get them to leave the country; they must be allies of the terrorists David had been assigned to stop. And it must have been Sharifa who had put the note in April's backpack. She felt a chill rush over her body. She knew she couldn't stop Minkabh. But maybe, somehow, she could still help David. After Minkabh left, she could go into the tombs and find him.

Minkabh fumbled with the latch on the gate, and April heard the lock shut with a dull click. How could she get in now? She watched as he stumbled to the car, got inside, and started the engine. Then he lurched back toward the road. April wondered if he'd be able to make it that far, let alone get back to the city, but swerving and weaving, he was soon out of sight.

She was truly alone. "David!" she called. "David!" There was no answer.

But she *wasn't* alone. The ghost by the gate was standing now, and April could see that it was a man. "Who are you?" she asked.

"I am one of the dead." The voice was low, hollow, matter-of-fact.

April felt another chill. "You mean you live in the Necropolis?"

The man nodded, then replied in broken English. "Police do not come here—so we make our own. Tonight, I guard this border." He flicked on his flashlight, revealing his ragged clothes, his sallow complexion.

"I need help," April said. "My husband is inside, and I have to get him out."

The man shrugged. "The gate is locked."

"There must be another way in."

The man paused. "No. There is no other way."

"I don't believe you." April looked him in the eye. "Please. I have a friend here—maybe you know her."

The man laughed. "You have a friend here? I do not think so."

"Her name is Eshe."

The man opened his eyes in recognition, then nodded. "Yes, I know her." He started to smile. "You are the food woman—the American angel."

April nodded. "I brought food, yes. I was going to bring more—"

The man held up his hand. "It is all right. I will help you." He paused. "There is another way."

❧

The man took her farther north, an additional fifteen-minute walk along the side of the ragged cliffs. April was beginning to wonder if the man really intended to help her. Maybe, she thought, he had more sinister motives in mind. But he kept moving ahead through the darkness, finally stopping at some enormous boulders standing like sentinels at the cliff base. "Do you see?" he asked.

"Just boulders."

"Come." The man squeezed through a narrow opening between two of the boulders on the right. April followed close behind. He passed several more rocks and took a left turn after a boulder close to the cliff wall. Then he stopped. "Do you see?"

April looked down. At the base of the cliff was a hole. Reaching to her knees, it was just wide enough for one person to climb through. "Is that it?"

The man nodded. "Be careful." He put out his hand. "Take my flashlight."

"What about you?"

"I have another." He reached into his pocket, pulled out the light, and flicked it on.

"You won't come with me?"

"No. I must guard. Also," he said with a smile, "there are ghosts."

April shook her head. "If you won't come in here, how do you know about it?"

"Many know; only a few dare to enter. They go in and steal small artifacts. Sell them. But the punishment for stealing is very bad. Also, the work is dangerous." The man looked at her intently. "Some have not come out again." He paused. "My brother . . ."

April nodded. "I'm sorry. Thanks for your help."

"You are welcome. I'm told the drop into the tombs is not large. But again, be careful. And may God preserve you."

❧

Alone now, April got down on her knees and shined the flashlight into the hole, which was partly covered with a spiderweb. Holding the flashlight with the tips of her fingers, she used it to brush the web aside. Then she jumped as a spider, black with white markings, scurried across the edge of the hole and down into the tomb.

Great, she thought. *I have to go feet-first into a dark hole with a spider.* But she took a deep breath and backed into the opening, feeling for the floor with her feet. Nothing but air. How deep was this thing? Cautiously, using the flashlight to see, she turned her head and looked down. The floor was about three feet below her. Relieved, she half-slid, half-dropped the rest of the way into the tomb, wondering how she was going to get out again later.

The room was dusty and nondescript—probably emptied by looters long ago. Hoisting her backpack higher onto her shoulders, she passed through a doorway at the end of the room, stepping into a long, narrow passageway. She was about to continue when she had a thought. Removing her backpack, she rummaged through the big pocket, taking out her map of Cairo and a felt-tip pen. On the back of the map, she drew a small square and wrote "Entrance" next to it, then drew a short line representing the hallway. If she kept on like this, she reasoned, she should have no trouble finding her way back. The hard part would be finding David. She hoped she wasn't too late.

David had been trying to sleep, but every time he drifted off, his hands would go numb, and he'd wake up again. He'd never understood before how cruel it was to tie someone's hands. It was worse than uncomfortable—it was maddening. If he could just get off the altar, he could probably find a way to break the plastic ties. But the nylon rope made that impossible.

He looked over at the flashlight. Its power was nearly gone, its once-bright light now a dusty yellow. As the light waned, the gleam of the golden artifacts around him turned muddy gray, their magnificence melting into shadow.

My life, too, he reflected. *We work so hard to accomplish something—anything—thinking it will give meaning to our existence, hoping somehow it will make us live forever.*

And how long, really, would it last? How many Egyptian kings had spent their whole lives trying to ensure their immortality, only to have their monuments smashed to rubble by succeeding rulers or worn to dust by the sands of time? And so it would go till the end of the world.

Vanity, vanity, all is vanity, he thought, remembering Ecclesiastes.

Then he felt a surge of anger, a kind of sharp determination welling up inside him. *If I get out of here,* he thought, *things will be different.* He was dismayed at what he'd considered important—getting a promotion, moving up in the bureau, "getting ahead." Ahead of what? And why did it matter?

The problem wasn't that he'd placed his ladder on the wrong wall; the problem was thinking that he'd had to climb a ladder in the first place—and look where it had brought him. Of course he had to support his family, but that was something different—a matter of faith, of consecration. Satan's lie wasn't just that anything could be bought with money; it was that those were the only things worth having.

Choking back a sob, David felt to his core the insidiousness of that lie. He wouldn't fall for it again.

From now on, he thought, *I'll focus on what really matters—God, family, service. Those will be the reasons behind everything I do.* He'd made that promise before, in the temple. This time, with a deeper understanding, he made it in his heart.

CHAPTER 16

"As they lifted up their hands upon me, that they might offer me up and take away my life, behold, I lifted up my voice unto the Lord my God, and the Lord hearkened and heard, and he filled me with the vision of the Almighty, and the angel of his presence stood by me, and immediately unloosed my bands."—Abraham 1:15

April looked at her watch. It was nearly seven in the morning; she'd been searching all night. The tomb complex was much bigger than she'd imagined. Even so, all of the rooms she'd seen so far had been empty—evidently areas archaeologists had already cleared. Her map was becoming fairly complex, and there were still plenty of passageways she hadn't explored, knowing she might have to come back to them if her current route didn't pan out. She'd marked these on her map, and at every juncture, she'd called out for David, then waited, listening, hoping. But the only response had been the dull silence of the tombs.

She had to rest—at least for a few minutes. She was exhausted, and her feet hurt from walking on the stone floors. She took off her backpack and removed her shoes, then sat in the passageway, bowing her head to pray. "Please," she said, "I'm so tired. Please give me strength. Please watch over David and help me find him."

As she whispered the words, she felt a warmth slip over her, a feeling that things *would* work out, that David was all right—and that it was all right to rest. She placed her flashlight carefully onto the floor and then, with a deep breath, pressed the switch. The darkness was instant, thick, almost palpable. She brought her hand up within inches of her face, but she couldn't see a thing.

She should have been frightened, but somehow she wasn't—not anymore. She thought of the psalm: "Though I walk through the valley of the shadow of death, I will fear no evil: for thou art with me." The words filled her with comfort and peace, and she repeated them over and over, feeling the reality of their meaning, until, finally, she fell asleep.

❧

"So you've come to report," Baruti said. He smoothed back his thick, white hair, then looked intently at Minkabh.

"Yes."

"Everything went as it should?" The man took a puff on his *shisha*.

"Yes."

"You are not saying much. Is your American friend actually dead?"

"Ah. Well. Not exactly."

Baruti put down the mouthpiece to his *shisha*. "I thought we could count on you."

"He'll be dead soon enough. I left him tied up in the tombs."

"And if he escapes?"

Minkabh felt a surge of anger. "How could he escape?"

"I don't know. But I do know it is a mistake to leave loose ends, however tight you *think* they might be."

"He will not escape; he will die, in the darkness."

"Yes, he likely will." Baruti picked up his mouthpiece and took another puff. "But I had thought, Minkabh, that we could count on you to finish a job."

"I did what I thought was best."

"You gave in to your own cowardice."

Minkabh thrust out his chest. "I am not afraid."

"No? Then show me." The man paused, narrowing his eyes. "Bring me the head of this David Hunter."

The big man stared. "What? You must be joking."

"Can you think of a better way to prove your courage? Your loyalty?"

Minkabh looked away.

"Your problem, Minkabh, is that you have always tried to accommodate two different worlds. You have never fully chosen one or the other. But today, *now,* you must choose. Where does your loyalty lie? With the American dogs? Or with your people, your family? Your son?"

Minkabh stood stiffly, his lips tight, his eyes red. "My son," he said hoarsely. "I choose my son."

"Good. If that is true, you will do what I have asked. If you fail . . . Well, it would be better for you—and your family—if you did not."

Minkabh grimaced, breathing hard. "My family has *nothing* to do with this."

Baruti's eyes narrowed. "Under the circumstances, they have *everything* to do with this. They are what matters most to you. This, too, is part of choosing. You may as well learn that now."

Minkabh shook his head. "You are a hard man, Baruti."

"I do what I must to achieve the ends I seek. You must do the same. There is no other way."

"What would you have me do?"

"You must attack violently with the knife, without thought of what you are doing; you must cut as you would the throat of a sheep or goat, but more deeply, through muscle and tissue clear to the bone. Then it is a simple matter to sever the vertebrae with a final pull of the blade." The man blew a cloud of smoke into the air. "Do you understand?"

"Yes." His face was grim.

Baruti nodded. "Good. Then I will know with certainty where you stand. Now act quickly."

After Minkabh left, Baruti signaled to the guard, who left for a minute, then came back with the American woman—so dark, so beautiful, so enticing. *Truly,* he thought, looking her over, *youth is wasted on the young. They have no idea of their own power.*

"So," Baruti said. "You are having second thoughts."

Pam nodded. "I've decided I can't lower the barricades for you. I want out."

"And what has changed?" He took a puff from his *shisha.*

"David."

"Your partner."

"Yes. He's just so—so *good.*"

"You have been unable to distract him."

She shook her head. "This has never happened before. I don't understand."

The old man chuckled. "That is because you are corruptible—and therefore you think everyone else must be corruptible. But that is not so. The mighty of the world—those like myself—know who they are and what they are about. They are true to their own hearts. You have found such a man in David Hunter. Yes, he is our enemy, and I will be glad to see him dead. But at least we know where he stands."

"I see."

The man narrowed his eyes. "One must choose, once and for all, the side on which one will fight. As your Christian Bible says, a double-minded man is unstable in all his ways. He cannot be depended on. He cannot even depend on himself."

"You're right. I understand."

"Good." The man paused. "So, you say you cannot lower the barricades."

"No. Nekhbet was assigned to come with me—to make sure I did what I was supposed to do. She can lower the barricades. I won't get in the way."

"Perhaps not. But this assignment was a test, to prove your loyalty and ensure your allegiance in the future. Unfortunately, your failure to follow through reveals your instability; we no longer know *what* you might do. So we must make sure you will not be a problem." He signaled to the guard. "Take her away."

The guard stiffened. "And kill her?"

Baruti paused. "Not yet. She may still be useful, if she can settle her loyalties correctly. If not . . ." He looked at Pam meaningfully, then nodded. "For now, just make sure she doesn't get away."

❧

President Morales looked out the tinted side window of the big black limousine as it pulled up to the guardhouse. Her driver spoke briefly with the guard, who lowered the security barriers. Then the driver pulled up in front of the embassy and helped the president out of the car, Secret Service agents at her side.

Only five feet tall and weighing no more than a hundred pounds, the president was famous for her fierce temper and no-nonsense style. In spite of her tiny stature, she'd risen rapidly through the ranks of power, starting as a Texas legislator, then capturing the office of governor, and finally being elected president as an independent candidate by U.S. voters, who decided they'd had enough nonsense from both Democrats and Republicans and were determined to try something completely new.

Now she gazed up at the blocky limestone building, wondering how the United States had ever managed to build something so ugly. But it wasn't the building's appearance that bothered her; it was what had been happening here for far too long. It was time to clean up the mess, once and for all. If Ambassador Hodges wasn't going to do it, she'd find someone who would. It was time to make him squirm. Her face grim, she stalked through the embassy doors.

When April opened her eyes, she was surprised at the darkness. Remembering where she was, she reached down for her flashlight. It wasn't there. Fighting off panic, she felt the floor around her, but without success. She realized she must have changed positions while she was sleeping, so she knelt on the floor and systematically felt to the edge of the hallway on each side, moving forward a few inches at a time. Finally, her fingers located her shoes and then her backpack. Next to the backpack was her flashlight, which she switched on with a quick prayer of gratitude. The beam seemed weaker; it wouldn't last forever. She'd need to be careful. And she'd need to find David—soon.

She stood and dusted herself off, feeling much better than when she'd sat down. Then she looked at her watch—seven minutes till nine. She'd slept nearly two hours. She put on her shoes, ate a banana, and drank some water. Then she put on her backpack and began walking down the passageway. But after several hundred feet, she paused. Had she been here before? Or was this new? Was she even going the right way? She looked at her map, but it offered no help. The hallway looked exactly the same in each direction, and she no longer knew on which side she'd been sleeping. Both, she supposed. She was about to turn back, but was back really back, or was it forward?

She was ready to throw up her hands and just start walking when she remembered the army knife with its tiny compass. She fished it out of her backpack and looked at the needle. The hallway ran north and south. She'd entered on the west side of the tomb complex—at least that's where the gate was—but now that she thought about it, the entrance had been farther north where the cliffs curved around, so maybe she'd come in from the north. Or the northwest—she didn't really know. Which meant she had no way to figure out with any certainty whether she was going in the right direction. Without knowing her starting point, the compass was useless. She was lost. And she was fed up with this whole thing.

"David!" she screamed. "David, where are you?"

She stopped, listening. Nothing but silence. But she wouldn't find him by standing still; she had to move forward, in one direction or the other.

After all, she thought grimly, *I have a fifty-fifty chance of being right.*

❧

An hour later, April was still looking, but the darkness and the silence—and her fears—were starting to get the better of her.

I should have found him by now, she thought. *I must have gone in the wrong direction.* But then a new thought struck her: *Maybe he's already dead.* The idea filled her with terror. "David! Answer me!" She was shouting as loud as she could, but her voice sounded small and flat in the narrow passageway.

"David!" She closed her eyes, listening again. And this time, she heard something. It was a voice. A still, small voice. It was David's voice. And he was calling her name.

"April!" The sound came from far away, as if in a dream.

"David! David! Is that you?" She choked back a sob, wiping the tears from her cheeks.

"April! Help me!"

She turned in the direction of the voice, began running down the passageway. "David! Keep yelling! I'm coming!"

His voice grew louder, warmer. Finally, she turned a corner, and suddenly things began to look familiar. Shining her flashlight into the rooms along this new hallway, she saw furniture, statues, the glint of gold.

"David!" she called.

And then, there he was, fastened to the altar. And very much alive.

"Oh, David," she said. She kissed him on the forehead, then opened the army knife, hacking through the nylon ropes and slicing through the plastic ties.

He sat up, rubbing his wrists, the tears streaming down his face. "Thank you," he said. "Thank you." He grabbed her and pulled her to him, kissing her over and over. For a long time they said nothing, simply holding each other in the darkness.

"April," he finally said, "I'm so sorry—"

"Shhh," she said, putting her finger to his lips. "It's okay. I'm sorry too. But we can talk about that later. Right now, we need to get out of here."

But how? And in what direction? April had no idea.

⁂

Minkabh stepped out of the big Mercedes and looked cautiously around. Seeing no one, he pulled out his keys, unlocked the gate, and stepped through. Then, with a clang, he shut the gate behind him.

He knew he needed to finish his assignment, but his heart felt like lead in his chest, heavy with the things he had done—and with the things he was about to do. But it didn't matter; he had made his decision. He would kill the American, just as he had promised. But he knew that his heart would be dead for the rest of his days.

Taking a flashlight from the back of the wooden door, he entered the waiting darkness.

❧

The guard had taken Pam to the back room of a coffeehouse, where he'd tied her to a chair. But on the way, she'd been able to do a little damage. The man was ugly enough already, with his yellow teeth and pockmarked complexion, but now his eye was turning a deep shade of purple where she'd hit him with her elbow. He kept glaring at her as he sipped his coffee.

At least she was still alive. But she wouldn't be for long, she knew, unless she joined the terrorists once and for all—or at least made them think that's what she had done. But they would always require proof—something she might not be able to give. She shook her head at her own indecision. Why couldn't she just *commit,* one way or the other?

She kept thinking about what Baruti had said to her: *The mighty of the world know who they are and what they are about. They are true to their own hearts.*

Had she ever been true to anything? *To my husband,* she thought. But even that wasn't true. Her work, her desire to get ahead, had always come first. *One must choose, once and for all, the side on which one will fight.* The idea of actually *taking* a side was a little new to her. But, as she was beginning to understand, it was something she couldn't avoid forever. Life required choices. And now, her life depended on her making a choice. With that thought, she made her decision. She looked over at the guard, determination welling up inside her.

"You know," she said, "I didn't mean to hurt you; it wasn't personal."

The man grunted. He didn't look all that bright.

"Do you have a family?"

"No."

"A girlfriend?"

The man glared at her. "No."

"What are you going to do with me?"

"That depends, I guess." He looked toward the door.

She paused. "I know one thing we could do—while we're waiting."

"What?"

"Come over here."

"Why?"

"I want to be close to you." She gave him her most seductive smile.

"You're tied up."

"I don't have to be."

"You'll try something."

"No, I won't—I promise." She paused. "I figure if I'm nice to you now, you'll be nice to me later. Isn't that right?"

"Maybe." The man shrugged. But he was starting to look interested.

"You won't be sorry."

"What are you going to do?"

"Come here and I'll show you." She tilted her head.

The man took a knife from the table. "If you try anything, I'll cut your pretty face." He stood and walked over; then he knelt down and severed the rope holding her right hand.

Pam lifted her hand, gently touching his cheek. "You poor thing; you're really hurt." She moved her fingers up and down, brushing his face. Then she moved down to his neck. She opened the top button on his shirt and put her hand on his chest.

"The room's locked," the man said, breathing heavily.

"I know." She smiled, touching his lips.

He stood, undoing the rest of his buttons.

"Wait," she said.

"What?"

"I need to go to the bathroom first. Then I'll come out. Okay?"

"Okay," he said. "But hurry. And remember—I have a knife."

"I know. I'll be fast."

He cut the ropes holding her to the chair, and she walked to the bathroom door, looking back over her shoulder with a smile. "While I'm in here," she said, "why don't you finish getting undressed?"

She ducked into the bathroom, closing the door behind her. Sure enough, the room had a window—and it was even open, just waiting for her to escape.

Minutes later, two men from the council entered the back room of the coffeehouse. The guard was naked. And the prisoner was gone.

"Do you know your way out?" April asked.

David shook his head. "I was relying on Minkabh."

"Not a good idea."

"No. Next time I'll keep my eyes open."

"Let's never have a next time."

"Good idea." He looked at his watch, then looked up in alarm. "It's after eleven!"

"I had to sleep—"

"No, you don't understand. They're going to bomb the embassy at noon!"

"Who? Minkabh?"

"Or someone he works with." He quickly told her the whole story.

"Can't you call on your cell phone?"

"Down here? Not likely." He pulled the phone out of his pocket and flipped it open, then shook his head. "No signal."

"We need to get outside."

Back in the hallway, they tried to get their bearings. "I'm sure Minkabh came in from the right," David said. "After that, I don't know. Maybe we can tell when we see it."

They moved along the passageway, with April shining her flashlight ahead of them. Then she paused. "David, look."

"What?"

"Footprints."

In the dust on the floor, several sets of prints were clearly evident. One of them was David's.

"Looks like I've been here before," he said with a smile.

"David, this is great! We can follow these out of here."

David nodded. He felt hope rising inside him. "Maybe we can even get out in time." He looked at his watch. "But we'll be cutting it awfully close."

❧

Runihura parked his bus on the side of the road, two blocks away from the American embassy, and watched the minutes tick past, one by one, on the dashboard clock. Seven minutes until noon. He looked back at the steel drums that filled the bus, his eyes shining with pride—and with terror at what he was about to do.

Over the months, he had gathered the necessary materials, finally filling each drum with a mixture of fertilizer, fuel oil, and rocks—a lethal combination. Now the day had come—the time for which he had so long waited and prepared. At last, the American presence in his country would be destroyed, the infidels—including the American president!—sent to eternal torment. The thought sent a thrill through his entire body. It would be a fitting punishment for their constant, arrogant interference in affairs that were not their own. His life was a small price to pay; his fame—and his reward—would be everlasting. He closed his eyes, imagining the crystal waters, the verdant gardens, the sweet fruits of paradise. And the women! The shy, slender virgins, eager to gratify his every desire.

The horn of a passing car broke his reverie. Two minutes. It was time to move. He took a deep breath, then looked out at the glowing flowers, the blue, blue sky. Suddenly, he was filled with ecstasy. All of his cares, all of his restraints, melted into nothingness. Like a mighty bull, he was full of strength. Like a stone mountain, he was invincible. He was free!

Heedless of everything around him, he started the engine and shifted the bus into gear. It moved slowly at first, but as he pressed down the accelerator, it gradually began picking up speed. He shifted gears, the engine roaring, then shifted again. The bus was moving quickly now, gaining momentum, the trees and pedestrians flying by at a prodigious rate. He kept his foot on the accelerator, his hands on the wheel.

Ahead of him was the guardhouse, with the barriers lowered—all according to plan. But something was wrong—the barriers were starting to come up again. He looked into the guardhouse. As planned, the guards were gone. But behind the heavy glass window he could see two women, and they appeared to be fighting—not just with words but with fists. What was going on?

To his relief, the barriers went back down. But the fight wasn't over. The smaller woman elbowed the taller woman in the face, and they both went down, the taller woman pulling the other one down with her. But the way was clear. He forced the accelerator all the way to the floor, exhilarated—and terrified—at how fast he was going.

Then, suddenly, the barriers were coming back up. And this time, he could see, they weren't going to stop. They emerged like rockets from their housing in the concrete, their metallic bulk moving up and up and up. He stomped on the brakes, but the bus plunged forward, its dangerous mass far too great to control in so short a time.

The barriers were before him, confronting him like sentinels, looming larger and larger until they crashed through the front of the bus with a shriek of tearing metal and breaking glass. Then came a deeper sound, a roar of fire and thunder, and the whole world collapsed into darkness.

David and April hurried down the hallway following the footprints, actually making good progress now that they knew where they were going. But the tunnels seemed to go on forever. As they came around a corner, the air seemed fresher, the rooms along the passageway more familiar.

"I think we're getting close," April said. "Good thing, too—this flashlight won't last much longer."

David nodded, then looked at his watch. "It's almost noon," he said. He looked up, his face white. "I don't think we're going to make it."

As he finished speaking, he heard a low rumble in the distance. "Wait," he said, clutching April's arm. "Listen."

"What *is* that?" April asked. The rumble grew louder, more menacing. It was getting worse; it was getting *closer*. The blood drained from her face. "It's an earthquake. We've got to get out of here."

David shook his head. "I don't think so. They've bombed the embassy."

"No," April breathed. "All those people . . ."

But as they listened, something else started to happen. The rumble increased in intensity, and then the floor began to tremble under their feet.

"It's not a bomb, David. It *is* an earthquake." April looked up at the massive stone blocks above their heads. Dust drifted from the cracks onto the floor.

As quickly as it had started, it was over. The ground was quiet. An eerie stillness filled the tomb.

"What happened?" April put her hand against the stone wall.

"I think you were right—it *was* an earthquake." David paused. "Do you think a bomb could *start* an earthquake?"

April shook her head. "I don't know. Maybe if the earthquake was overdue anyway."

They turned to leave, but suddenly the very air seemed to explode, and the floor gave a giant heave, throwing them both to their knees. The rumble returned, deafening in its intensity, and they staggered to their feet, their hands over their ears. Chunks of rock fell from the ceiling in the hallway ahead, and with a thunderous crash, an entire stone block fell, then another, and another. Dust and debris rained down everywhere.

"Run!" David yelled. He grabbed April's hand, pulling her back into the tombs. Behind them, he could hear the roof collapsing, the walls caving in. Ahead of them, the floor began to buckle, the walls heaving up and down. David kept falling and getting up, falling and getting up, fearing every moment they'd be crushed by the massive stones overhead. Through the dust, he could see April struggling along next to him. He reached for her hand but couldn't get to her—everything kept *moving* so violently.

Finally, after what seemed like hours, the shocks began to diminish. And then, with a last, giant wheeze, the shaking stopped, the rumbling ceased. David looked over at April. She was gasping for breath, trembling with terror, and her hands and knees were bleeding. But she was still standing. David struggled to get up but couldn't—the pain in his left foot was too great.

I'm hurt, he thought. *But at least we're alive.*

They certainly wouldn't be getting out of the tombs the way they'd hoped. Maybe now they wouldn't be able to get out at all.

CHAPTER 17

"The records of the fathers, even the patriarchs, concerning the right of Priesthood, the Lord my God preserved in mine own hands; therefore a knowledge of the beginning of the creation, and also of the planets, and of the stars, as they were made known unto the fathers, have I kept even unto this day, and I shall endeavor to write some of these things upon this record, for the benefit of my posterity that shall come after me."—Abraham 1:31

David looked down at his ankle, which was swollen to twice its normal size. "I sprained it," he said. "I'm sorry."

"Like you had any control over it." April had cleaned the blood and grime off her hands and knees, and now she was working on David. "Wow, that looks bad. Take your shirt off."

"What?"

"Take your shirt off. I'm going to wrap your ankle. Maybe you'll be able to walk."

David unbuttoned his shirt and handed it to April, grimacing with pain. "Do you have to wrap it so tight?"

"That's kind of the point, isn't it?"

"I guess."

She helped him up, but he couldn't stand alone. With her support, he was able to take a few steps, but pain shot up his leg with each move forward.

"Can you do this?" she asked.

"I don't have much of a choice, do I?"

"Not really."

"You can't lean on me forever; we'll need to find you a walking stick."

"Good idea." David shined the flashlight back into the passageway where they'd been—the hallway leading out of the tombs. It didn't take more than a glimpse to see that it was completely blocked with rubble. And that meant they had to find another way out. But where?

"We need to think about this," David said. "What have we got?"

April dug through her backpack. "We still have two bottles of water and two oranges. Here's my crummy map and felt-tip pen. We have your triple combination and this little New Testament I bought at the bazaar. Plus the army knife, which ought to come in handy somehow. Oh, and Donkor's flashlight—which doesn't work."

"Shoot," David said. "What's wrong with it?"

"I don't know. Batteries, probably. He got it out of his glove compartment."

David picked it up. "It's a cheap flashlight. Maybe it's the switch."

"Maybe."

He flicked the switch several times without success, then unscrewed the top and pulled out the batteries.

"Shall we see if they're good?"

"Okay. But it's going to be awfully dark while you make the switch. Make sure you don't drop anything."

"We do have my cell phone."

"It doesn't work."

"But it makes a pretty decent makeshift flashlight." He pulled it out of his pocket and opened it.

"Oh, good idea."

He handed it to April, then turned off the working flashlight. The light from the cell phone was dim, but he could still see what he was doing. Quickly, he took the batteries from the good flashlight and replaced them with the ones from Donkor's light. Then he screwed the top back on and flicked the switch.

Nothing.

"Great," April said.

David angrily whacked the flashlight against his palm. For a split-second, the light flickered on, then back off.

"Whoa!" David said. "We've got something." He took out the batteries again and examined them in the light of the cell phone. "They're kind of dirty," he said. "We need some sandpaper."

"Sorry, I'm fresh out," April said. "How about sand?"

David laughed. "That ought to work."

April bent down and swept some sand from the floor into her hand, then held it out to David, who rubbed the ends of the batteries with it until they were shining and clean. He put them into the flashlight and turned on the switch.

A beam of golden light flooded the passageway.

"Oh, that's nice," David said.

"Better than nice. It could save our lives."

David nodded. "We'll save the old batteries for later—just in case. What else do you have in your magic backpack?"

"That's it. But the army knife has a little flashlight—it's a good one, too." She pulled it out of its slot and switched it on. The tiny beam cut through the darkness like a blade.

"Light-emitting diodes," David said. "Nice."

"There's also a compass." She turned the knife over, showing the tiny instrument embedded in the plastic.

"Well, at least we can tell which direction we're going. Maybe we can keep from going back over the same ground."

"Right." April thought a moment. "You know," she said, "there's another thing. The Egyptians thought of these tombs as temples, and they'd go through them from west to east, toward the direction of the sunrise. So to get out, we should probably try going east."

David smiled. "It's nice being married to someone so smart."

"Don't you forget it," she said.

"Never again. Oh, and April?"

"Yes?"

"I really do like the knife you bought me."

She laughed. "I thought maybe you could use it."

It would be nice, David thought, *if we could actually find an east-west passage.* So far, they'd been stuck in a hallway running from north to south, at least according to the compass. The earthquake had done a lot of damage, and sometimes they had to scramble over blocks of stone or squeeze past piles of debris. David feared that the *other* end of the hall might be blocked as well, and if it was, getting out probably wouldn't be possible—a thought he tried to push out of his mind. But so far, they'd managed to keep going, although his ankle was still giving him a lot of trouble and he'd had to lean on April all the way.

As they kept moving forward, the damage from the earthquake began to lessen, but David noticed that the ceiling seemed to be getting lower, the walls closer together. Not only that, but up ahead he spotted a wall—the tunnel was coming to an end. "I hate to say it," David said, "but—"

"Yeah, I see it."

He stopped. "We're going to have to turn around and go back."

"Not yet we aren't. And besides, there's nowhere else to go."

"We don't know that," David said. "Maybe there's a passage we overlooked."

"Maybe. But we're already here. Let's go as far as we can. Then we can decide what to do. Maybe there'll be an opening of some kind."

"I hope so."

As they approached the end of the tunnel, David could see that April was right. The tunnel had been purposely narrowed to make it *look* as though it were coming to an end, but just before they came to the wall, the tunnel took a sharp turn to the right.

"Pretty neat," David said. "How did you know?"

"I didn't. I just don't like giving up."

David kissed her. "You know," he said, "you're all right—in spite of what people say."

"Humph," April said. "Very funny."

David shone the flashlight into the dark passageway, but it was impossible to see where it led. "At least we'll be going east," he said.

❧

After several minutes of painful walking, David could see another wall ahead. "Here we go again," he said.

"You hope. Maybe this time there won't be a way out."

"Let's go as far as we can. Maybe there'll be an opening of some kind."

"Cute," April said.

"I like to think so."

As they reached the wall, they found another corridor branching off to the right—going back the way they'd already come.

David groaned. "Great," he said. "We're headed back where we started."

April frowned, narrowing her eyes. "I don't think so. I think I know what this is. It's a labyrinth."

"What?"

"A labyrinth. It's like a maze. I saw one in the cathedral at Chartres."

"If it's a maze, we may never find our way out."

April shook her head. "You can't get lost in a labyrinth. There aren't any side routes or dead-ends. If you just keep going, eventually you'll get out."

"What's the point, then?"

"It's a metaphor for life. We're born, we move through the twists and turns of mortality, and finally we die and come out on the other side."

"Like the temple again."

"Exactly."

Half an hour later, David wondered how long the labyrinth could keep going. All of the walking back and forth, around and around, was getting to be a bit disorienting. And his leg was giving him fits. The tunnels did seem to be getting shorter, but at the same time they were getting narrower, and the ceiling was becoming alarmingly low.

Occasionally David looked over at April to see how she was doing. She seemed fine, but she was having a hard time walking while hunched over so much. Finally, they had to get down on their hands and knees—something that didn't help the pain in his leg. "Are you okay?" he asked.

"I'm worried. If this keeps up, we'll be crawling along on our stomachs pretty soon. And what if the tunnel gets too narrow to go through?"

"That's what I've been worrying about."

April paused. "Maybe this is part of the lesson the Egyptians were trying to teach—that we won't get through life without learning humility, without prostrating ourselves before the gods."

"I hope you're right. Because if we have to go back, we'll be in trouble."

"We're already in trouble."

For a moment, David was silent. "I know."

"Let's just keep going forward. I don't know what else to do."

"We can pray again. We're already on our knees."

"I've *been* praying."

"Me too. But we can pray out loud—together."

April nodded her head. "You go first."

⁂

At least, David thought as he pulled himself along with his elbows, *I don't have to use my leg.* But they'd already had to rest many times; crawling through the dust on the cold stones was amazingly tiring. "How do babies do this?" he asked.

"They're smaller. And younger. And they don't have so far to go." April coughed. "I'm sick of this dust."

"Me too." Then he paused, listening. He turned off the flashlight.

"What's wrong?"

"I thought I heard something."

Together they lay in the darkness, trying not to breathe. In the distance they heard a scraping sound, like the opening of a door.

"I think someone is in here," April whispered.

"Maybe. It could be a rat."

"It could be someone coming to rescue us!"

"I don't think we're that lucky."

David heard the sound of footsteps approaching and saw the beam of a flashlight moving in the room ahead. They'd reached the end of the tunnel. But there was no way David was going out.

"David," Minkabh called out. "Where are you? I'm sorry for what I did. I was wrong. I've come back to help you."

I don't think so, David thought, his heart in his throat. What if Minkabh saw the entrance to the tunnel and looked inside? *Please,* David silently prayed, *don't let him find us. Keep us safe.*

In the dim light from Minkabh's flashlight, David saw something moving. A tiny, black-and-white spider had spun a web across the tunnel opening and was going about its business, cleaning and repairing the strands in case some morsel of food should come along.

What we need is a wall, David thought gloomily. *A spiderweb isn't going to hide us.* He jumped as the flashlight's beam rested on the web. *We're dead,* he thought. But, to his surprise, the beam slowly moved on, and David listened as Minkabh's voice faded into the distance, calling their names. *Why didn't he look in the tunnel?* David wondered. Then he understood: the spiderweb told Minkabh that no one had entered the tunnel in a long, long time. He simply hadn't thought it necessary to look inside.

Thank you, David prayed. *Thank you for watching over us.* He thought of the Book of Mormon: *By small and simple things are great things brought to pass.* Truly, the Lord was wiser than the most intelligent of men.

CHAPTER 18

"I have long held the view that the universe is built on symbols whereby one thing bespeaks another; the lesser testifying of the greater, lifting our thoughts from man to God, from earth to heaven, from time to eternity."—Elder Orson F. Whitney, *Improvement Era*, 30:851

David felt bad about breaking through the spiderweb, but it was the only way out of the tunnel. Using the flashlight, he brushed the web to the side, being careful not to harm the spider, which went scurrying off into the darkness.

As they emerged from the tunnel, David swept the flashlight beam over the dusty floor. Minkabh's footprints were clearly evident; according to the compass, they were leading off to the west. David smiled and turned to April. "He's going the wrong way."

"Good. Maybe we have a chance of getting out of here alive."

As they walked eastward together, David thought how good it felt to be out of the tunnel. The crawling had been miserable, but at least it had given his leg a rest, and now it wasn't bothering him so much.

At first the hallway was fairly low and narrow, with occasional passageways running off to the north and south, but eventually the ceiling grew higher, the walls farther apart. After a time, it could no longer be called a passageway; it had definitely become a room.

But it was no ordinary room. The walls were covered with images and hieroglyphics in a breathtaking array of reds and oranges, purples and blues, all with shining highlights of gold. For several moments, David and April just stared. They'd never seen anything so magnificent.

"I think we've found your temple," David said.

April nodded. "I think you're right."

❦

David and April moved eastward through the temple, hoping they'd soon find the way out. But the wall paintings were magnificent, and David paused from time to time to look at some of them. In reality, he was resting his leg, trying to keep the pain at bay—something he didn't want April to notice.

"Okay, April, you're the expert. So who's this?" David said, pointing the flashlight at an enormous figure of a man with the head of an ibis, the sharp beak reaching down to his chest. He was carrying a papyrus scroll and pen.

"David, we don't have time for this."

"I know. Tell me just a little, and then we'll go."

April sighed. "I'm no expert, but I do know that's Thoth, the scribe of the gods. He's here to take notes, make sure everything's done just right, and accompany the dead people through the temple." She looked over at David. "That's you and me, in case you didn't know."

"Not yet it's not."

"It will be if we don't keep moving."

"Okay, okay. I actually do want to live." They walked out of the room and into a long passageway, with David grimly pushing himself forward.

"Don't worry," April said. "At the end of the ceremony we come alive again—we're resurrected. Reborn."

"Well, that's a relief. You mean we get out?"

April smiled. "Same thing."

The next room was equally magnificent, with a crescent moon in silver arching overhead on one wall and the sun in gold rising on the other. But it wasn't rising on its own; it was being pushed by an enormous beetle.

David looked up at the wall. "What *is* that thing?"

"It's a scarab," April said. "Every morning it rolls the sun back up from the underworld."

"Like a big ball of dung?"

"Exactly. See, what's dung good for?"

"Uh, fertilizer?"

"Yup. So it's a symbol of life coming out of something dead."

"Okay, I see."

"Look at that!" April pointed at the ceiling, high above their heads. Painted in deep blue, the stones were covered with silver stars, winking and sparkling in the beam from the flashlight.

"Wow. Sun, moon, and stars. The morning of creation."

"'In the beginning . . . ,'" April said.

"Do you think it's the same thing?"

April shrugged. "Why not?"

"It was a completely different religion. Wasn't it?"

"I'm not so sure. Remember the book of Abraham? Pharaoh tried to imitate the priesthood order—the temple. He tried 'diligently,' the book says. So all of this could be closer than we think."

David nodded. "If that's right, the next room should be a garden."

"Can we find out, please?"

The next room *was* a garden, but not one like David had ever seen. The walls were covered with pictures of fruit trees and palm trees filled with birds and monkeys. A band of blue with silver ripples ran all around the room.

"It's the Nile," David said. "It's Egypt." In the river was a hippopotamus and a crocodile. And on the wall was the figure of a serpent—a serpent with legs.

"You've got to be kidding," David said.

"Maybe it means something else."

"I don't know; look over there."

On the other wall was the form of a woman in a long robe. Her hair was down, and she was picking fruit from one of the trees.

"I can't believe it," David said.

"Well, it *is* a very old story."

The next room, David anticipated, would be lone and dreary. To his surprise, it was anything but.

On one wall were pictures of farmers plowing their fields, followed by ships transporting goods down the river. On the other wall, workers

were constructing a building, measuring blocks with a ruler and using a triangular level to set them accurately in place.

Tools for building, David thought. And then his eyes widened as he noticed a table filled with *real* tools made from wood and beautifully painted—a large drafting compass, a carpenter's square, and several others. But what really caught his eye was a measuring rod nearly as tall as he was and an inch thick. "There's my walking stick," he said, picking it up and running his hand over the smooth surface.

"Are you really going to take that?"

"You bet. I'll ask forgiveness later." He tried walking, using the stick for support. It felt strong, solid in his hand, and he found he could finally move around without April's support. On his own, he walked to the far wall, which was decorated with an image of the king and his soldiers driving their chariots into battle, bows and arrows at the ready. Industry and activity were everywhere. The whole room was a perfect depiction of life in ancient Egypt.

"It's the world we live in now," April said. "Our current state of existence."

David nodded. "Life is short—we need to go. I should do better now that I've got a stick. So what's next?"

April shook her head. "I have no idea."

Together they walked forward into the darkness.

CHAPTER 19

"O my heart which I had upon earth, do not rise up against me as a witness in the presence of the lord of things; do not speak against me concerning what I have done, do not bring up anything against me in the presence of the great god."—Egyptian Book of the Dead, chapter 30

The passageway seemed to go on forever, and, to make things worse, the floor was steeply slanted, leading constantly up. Even with the stick, David was having a hard time walking, but he was determined to keep going, in spite of the pain.

April noticed, though. "Let's stop. You need to rest."

"No I don't. I'm okay."

"You don't look okay. Your face looks awful."

"Thanks a lot."

"You know what I mean. Let's rest—just for a minute. I could use a breather myself."

Reluctantly, David put down his stick and sat on the floor, his injured leg out in front of him.

April sat down next to him. "Honestly, now. How bad is it?"

"Uh, well, pretty bad."

"Even with your stick?"

David nodded.

"I'm sorry," April said. "Maybe we should sleep—just a little."

"Do we dare?"

"Not really."

David shook his head. "You sleep while I watch. Mostly, I just need to rest my leg."

"Okay. Thanks."

He looked at his watch. "It's nearly four o'clock."

"I'm hungry."

"Me too. But we should wait a little longer if we can. We can eat after we've both slept a little. That will give us more strength to keep going."

"Okay."

"Ready?"

April nodded, and David switched off the flashlight. The darkness was oppressive. But at least they were together. He put his arm around April's shoulders, pulling her close. Soon she was sleeping while David stared into the darkness, listening for the sounds of scraping footsteps or opening doors. But he was so tired.

Maybe I could close my eyes for just a few minutes, he thought. After that, he knew no more.

❧

"April, wake up."

"What? What time is it?"

He turned on the flashlight, then looked away, waiting for his eyes to adjust. "It's after eight. We slept more than four hours."

"I thought you were keeping watch."

"Sorry. I couldn't stay awake."

April rubbed her eyes and stretched. "It's okay. We needed the rest. And now we need to eat. I'm starving." She paused. "Do you think Minkabh gave up and went home?"

"I doubt we're that lucky—but we *are* a long way from where he was." David shined the flashlight over the walls of the room around them. The images were like nothing else he'd ever seen.

April got out a bottle of water and started peeling an orange while David looked around. At the entrance, near where they were resting, was a picture of a god with the head of a jackal. He was leading a man in a white robe by the hand.

"Who's this?" David asked.

April looked up. "Anubis, god of the dead. He's leading the dead person into the judgment hall." She nodded, indicating the next part of the painting. "And there, on the scales, is the man's heart. It's being weighed against the feather of Ma'at, a symbol of goodness and truth. If the man has spent his life doing good, his heart will be lighter than the feather, and he'll get to move on."

"What's that weird creature there?"

"That's Ammit. She has the head of a crocodile and the legs of a lion and a hippopotamus."

"Impressive. She doesn't look very friendly."

April shook her head. "She isn't. If the dead man has spent his life doing evil, his heart will be heavier than the feather. Then Ammit will eat his heart, and the man will cease to exist."

"For people who wanted to live forever, that must have been pretty frightening."

"I think that's the idea. But look over there." She pointed at the figure of Anubis in the middle of the scale. "That's Anubis again. He's adding weight to the scales."

"He's *what?* That doesn't seem fair."

"It *isn't* fair. If it were, the dead man wouldn't get through."

"You mean he's *helping* the dead man? The dead man isn't good enough on his own?"

"That's right. He's adding weight to the side with the feather."

David could hardly believe what he was seeing. "It's the Atonement," he said.

April nodded. "In a different form. But the idea is similar."

"Wow." He looked over at April. "What's the matter?"

"Oh, nothing."

"Yes there is. What's wrong?"

She shook her head.

"You can tell me."

"Uh . . . well, I'd like to know, I guess."

"What?"

She paused, looking at the picture. Then she gave him a half-smile. "Is your heart pure?" She looked down.

"Oh, April." Tears sprang to his eyes, and he reached over and took her into his arms. "Yes, April," he said. "You don't need to worry. I love you so much." A few days ago, he would have said exactly the same thing. But now, in this strangest of places, he knew what it really meant—something for which he would always be grateful.

ɂ

Minkabh moved through the familiar passages, watching, listening. But all was silent, with no sign of the American. He was beginning to get uneasy.

He can't possibly have escaped, Minkabh thought. *Could he?* If he had, the consequences—for both him and his family—would be too terrible to contemplate. David had to be here somewhere—and he *would* find him.

He put his hand to the gash on his forehead. The earthquake had done its damage, knocking him unconscious for a while, and he'd awakened in a pool of blood, sick and shaken. He'd had to rest several hours before he felt ready to move again.

The big man shined his flashlight down the long, empty hallway. *I should have killed him in the beginning,* he thought. *I was weak. But now*—he took a deep breath, narrowing his eyes—*I am strong. I will find him. And this time, I will finish the job I was sent to do.*

But half an hour later, there was still no sign of his prey.

Maybe, he thought, *I'm looking in the wrong place.* He stopped, going over the passageways in his mind. Could he have missed one somehow? His eyes narrowed, and he turned and began walking in the opposite direction.

David and April shared the bottle of water and the orange, and when they were finished, David actually felt much better. His leg had stopped throbbing, although it was still sore, and with the help of his walking stick, he felt ready to move on. But first, he wanted to know about the room's final picture.

"Okay, so let's say the man's heart doesn't get eaten and he gets to go on. What happens next?"

"He moves over there."

"The hawk-headed god is Horus. He's presenting the dead man at the final curtain. Behind it is Osiris, the head of the gods. He's sitting on his throne, ready to receive the man into his royal court, where he'll be reborn as a god himself."

"Well, that sounds familiar."

"Yes, it does." She looked over at him. "And it also means we should be close to getting out!"

"Thank goodness."

Together they got up, then made their way along the passage until the judgment scene was behind them, into what they hoped was the final room on their long journey.

❧

The next room was different from the others. The walls were empty, and instead of one doorway at the end of the room, there were three.

"That's not good," David said. "How do we know which door to take?"

"Door number three." Then she whispered, "A new car!"

"Very funny. I'd settle for a way out of here. I'm tired of being dead."

"Me too."

As they approached the doors, they could see that there actually were decorations—but not on the walls; they were on the floor, with different pictures in front of each door.

"I think it's a test," David said. "You should know by the pictures which door to pick."

April nodded. "What if you get it wrong?"

"You come back out and try again?"

She shook her head. "I don't think so."

"You fall through the floor and get eaten by crocodiles?"

"That seems more likely."

"Now you're just trying to scare me."

She smiled. "We should have a look."

They walked up to the first doorway and shined the flashlight into the darkness.

"It's a hallway," David said. "I'll bet it goes back a long way."

"Probably."

They moved on to the other doors, both of which were the same; each one opened into a separate passageway.

"So," David said, "if you pick the wrong door, you might not know it until a long time later. You could end up anywhere."

April nodded. "This is serious. We'd better get it right."

"How?"

"I think we'd better ask for help on this one."

David nodded, then took her into his arms. "We should both pray; you go first."

"All right."

Together they asked for guidance, pled for protection, and prayed for David's leg to be healed. When they were finished, they looked at each other, hoping something had changed.

"Any ideas?" April asked.

David shook his head. "You?"

"Not really. Maybe the pictures would give us a clue."

"We don't even know what they mean. Do we?"

"We haven't really looked yet."

The pictures were typically Egyptian. In front of the first door was a star—similar to the stars they'd seen on the ceiling in other rooms.

In front of the second door was an eye.

But the picture in front of the third door gave them pause; it was composed of four separate symbols.

April shook her head. "Any ideas?"

David sighed. "Not really. The first picture is obviously a star, but I don't know what that means."

"Next is a wedjat-eye," April said. "And I *do* know what that means."

"What?"

"If it's a left eye, it's the moon. Remember?"

"Oh, right."

"So we have a star and a moon. Why doesn't the last door have a sun?"

"I don't know." Thinking of his research in the library, David studied the symbols. "Those upraised arms are the same as that 'standard' we saw in the book of Abraham. Remember?"

"That's right."

The other symbols looked familiar as well, but he couldn't quite place them. But maybe if he thought of them as Hebrew characters . . .

"You know," David said, "that repeated character, the upraised arms, is the same as the Hebrew letter *hey*, but in Hebrew it's upside down." Squatting on the floor, supported by his walking stick, he drew a letter in the dust.

"In its earliest form, it means 'exists.'"

He tilted his head, looking at the string of hieroglyphs. "In Hebrew, the letter *yodh* means 'hand,' so that could be the character on the right."

And then, with a rush of understanding, he had the rest. "In Hebrew, the straight line is *vav*, a nail or tent peg—something that holds things together. So it goes next."

"Then we have *hey* again."

April stared. "What does it mean?"

David shrugged. "It's the most famous Hebrew word there is. It's the tetragrammaton—the name of God."

"You're kidding."

"Nope. Look." Under the Hebrew letters, David wrote their English equivalents:

HVHY

Then he wrote them from left to right.

YHVH

"YaHVeH," April said.

"That's right. Jehovah."

"Not just the sun, but also the Son."

David nodded. "It means something like 'He exists and exists' or 'I am and am.' Remember, the Lord told Moses His name was 'I AM.'"

"Wow," April said. Then she touched David's shoulder. "You know . . ."

"What?" He looked up at her.

"From an Egyptian point of view, there's another way to look at it."

"You've learned that much Egyptian?"

"Not really. But why couldn't the characters mean exactly what they look like? The one on the right is a hand. Next are uplifted arms, meaning 'Pay attention,' 'Look,' or 'Behold.' After that comes a nail. Then there's 'Behold' again."

"So it's 'hand behold nail behold'?"

"Right. But in English we'd just say, 'Behold the hand; behold the nail.'"

For a long moment, David was silent. Then he said, "That's astounding. Can that be right?"

"It looks that way."

David pulled himself up. His eyes were full of tears. "Any question about which door we should take?"

April shook her head. "The Savior said, 'I am the way.'"

The door led to a passageway which, after a long walk, opened into a room. But this one was different from the others they'd been in—it was smaller and perfectly square, and the big stone blocks forming the floor made a checkerboard of black and white, with each square nearly a yard across. David counted eight rows of eight squares, just like a chessboard. Other than that, the room was empty—looted, probably—except for three steps leading up to a large, shallow alcove carved into the stone surface of the back wall.

"Maybe that's the way out," April said.

David shook his head. "It's one of those false doors we saw at the museum. Supposedly that's where the god comes out to greet the worshipers. But it doesn't really open; it's just a carving." He paused, looking down.

"So we're stuck in here? What are we supposed to do?"

"Go back and start over, I guess."

"No way." For a moment, April couldn't speak. "And besides," she finally said, "we could just end up being wrong again."

"I know." Weariness settled over him like a shadow, and his leg was starting to throb again. "Let's take another rest," he said. "I need to sit down."

He moved gingerly across the checkerboard, using his walking stick for support. But as he neared the stairs, the floor in front of him seemed to give way, and with a shout he jerked backward, falling heavily onto the stones.

"David, are you okay?"

"I think so." Painfully, using his stick for support, he got to his feet. "Man, that really hurt."

"What happened?"

"There's a hole in the floor; it's a trap." Carefully, he put the stick out and tapped the stones in front of him. Sure enough, one of the black ones was missing—something nearly impossible to detect by sight alone.

"It's a good thing you had your stick."

"I would have fallen in." He looked over at April. "Don't move; I'll come to you," he said. "Then we'll go to the stairs and sit down."

He crossed the floor slowly, testing each block before going forward. April shined the flashlight so he could see better, but he couldn't always tell what was in front of him. He finally reached her, and then, together, they made their way across the room. As they neared the hole, David paused. "Wait a minute. I want to look in."

"Be careful." She handed him the flashlight.

"Believe me, I will." After testing the squares around him, he lay on the floor, his head projecting over the opening.

"I want to see," April said.

"No, you don't. It's deep. And there are bones down there."

"Human bones?"

"Yup," he said, pulling himself up. "We're not the first ones to come through here—or try to, anyway. We need to be careful; this may not be the only hole in the floor."

April thought for a moment. "The white stones should be safe."

"Unless one of them is some kind of trigger."

"Great."

Together they crossed the remaining few stones, tapping as they went, fearing with each step that the floor would fall through or the ceiling come crashing down on their heads. But they reached the stairs safely. After brushing a thin layer of sand onto the floor, they sat on the steps, shared the last of the water, and ate the last orange.

"Time to retire the flashlight," David said solemnly. "It's almost done." He handed it to April, who pulled the army knife out of her backpack, retrieved the tiny red flashlight from its slot, and switched it on. The light was bright but pitifully small. She switched off the old flashlight and put it into her backpack. Then she switched off the light on the army knife.

"Hey!" David said.

"We're resting, remember? We'll save the light for later."

David awoke to the sound of steps on the stone floor, and to his surprise, a splash of light washed over the walls of the room.

"April!" he whispered. "Wake up!"

"Why? What's going on?" She shielded her eyes from the light.

A shadowy figure loomed out of the darkness.

"I'm sorry, David," Minkabh said. "I should have killed you at the beginning; then April would have been able to live. Now you'll both have to die."

"I don't think so."

"I must say, you haven't been easy to find."

"We had help."

Minkabh snorted. "Obviously not enough, because here I am."

"I thought you couldn't bring yourself to kill me," David said.

"Things have changed."

"I wouldn't advise coming over here."

"Why not? Are you going to fight me?" Minkabh pulled out his big clasp knife, which he opened with a click.

"If I have to. This time, I'll be ready." David reached for the army knife that April was holding and flicked open the blade. It looked enormous, glinting dully in the dim light.

April held up the walking stick, but David shook his head. "I won't need it."

Minkabh paused, thinking things over. "Well," he said, "that improves your odds. But still, it's hardly a fair fight. I'm nearly twice your size, and far more experienced."

"You're hurt."

"So are you."

"But I'm better trained. So you're right—not a fair fight. I definitely have the advantage. But you can still live—if you walk away."

The big man laughed. "I'm afraid you won't get off quite that easily. And your offer shows me the shallowness of your confidence." He began moving across the checkered floor toward him.

David could feel his heart beating. "Aren't you going to put down your flashlight?"

"I may need to club you with it."

"I thought we were friends."

"Blood is thicker than water."

"I'm warning you one last time—don't come over here."

But the man kept walking straight toward them over the black-and-white floor.

David held his breath, watching as Minkabh came to the hole—and then stepped smoothly to the side.

"Sorry to disappoint you," Minkabh said. "I've been here before." Then he laughed and stepped forward.

"It doesn't matter." David put the knife out in front of him, steadying himself for the fight. April crouched in the corner of the alcove, trying to stay out of the way.

As Minkabh reached the stairs, he swung at David with the flashlight, and as David jumped back, the big man instantly mounted the stairs and turned, his knife at the ready. David moved quickly to stand in front of April.

"Protecting your family," Minkabh said. "I respect that. And to protect *my* family, I must kill you." He lunged at David with his blade, but David pivoted lightly to the side, gripping Minkabh's outstretched wrist and stabbing as deeply as he could with his knife. Minkabh jerked back, then stumbled down the stairs, his eyes wide with astonishment, dark blood spurting from his arm.

"I told you not to fight me," David said.

"You arrogant pup. I'll take your head off."

But this time David moved first, drawing back his arm and hurling his knife directly at Minkabh's chest. The man lurched to the side, but not quickly enough; the blade sank deep into his left shoulder. But he was still standing, still dangerous. David had gambled—and lost. And now he had no weapon.

Howling with rage, Minkabh strode forward.

April suddenly moved, leaning from the stairs and shoving David's walking stick directly between the man's ankles. Then she pulled to the side as hard as she could.

Minkabh tripped and stumbled backward, coming down with a

thud on the hard, stone floor. He missed landing directly in the hole, but the momentum of his fall carried the enormous bulk of his torso backward into the gaping chasm, and his legs quickly followed, vanishing into darkness. His scream seemed to go on forever.

After many minutes of stunned silence, David finally spoke. "I can't believe it." He shook his head. "If you hadn't moved . . ."

April was still staring at the hole. "I . . . I . . ."

"You saved my life." He sat down next to her on the stone steps, put his arm around her, and kissed her on the cheek. She was shaking. "It's okay," he said, pulling her close. "It's over."

"I didn't mean to kill him." Tears fell from her eyes.

"I know. It's okay," he said again.

They sat for a moment in silence. David finally closed his eyes, holding April close in his arms. "'Though I walk through the valley of the shadow of death, I will fear no evil: for thou art with me,'" he quoted quietly. "I've read that psalm so many times before, but it's never meant so much to me as it does right now."

April closed her eyes and pressed her face into David's neck. Sobs shook her trembling body.

"'Thy rod and thy staff they comfort me,'" David whispered, his eyes fixed on the walking stick at their feet.

He pressed a kiss to April's forehead, and then closed his eyes in prayer.

He offered thanks that his life—and April's—had been spared. He prayed for guidance to find a way out of the darkness. And then he prayed for Minkabh, for his wife and daughter. He prayed that when Minkabh's heart was weighed on the scales of justice, that he would find mercy—and peace.

❧

After some time, April turned on the little flashlight and began moving around the stairs of the tomb, gathering up their things. She looked over at David. "What do we do now?"

"We have to go back; there's no other choice."

April shook her head. "I'm not going back."

"You want to stay here and die?"

"I want to get *out*." She lifted her head. "We've figured everything out the best we could. We've prayed. Now here we are, at the end of the line. This *has* to be the way out."

"Not if we got something wrong."

"You know, David, I've been thinking. Things aren't always as they seem. Sometimes there are meanings we don't get at first glance. And, after all, this *is* a temple."

David narrowed his eyes. "Do you know something I don't?"

April tilted her head. "Remember the sand we brushed off these steps? If there's no connection to the outside, how did the sand get in here?"

David shrugged. "There's sand all over in these tombs. Maybe it sifted in through the ceiling when the earthquake hit. Maybe looters tracked it in. Who knows?"

"I don't think so. I think this alcove isn't an alcove; I think this alcove is a *door*."

"No, it's not. Just look at it," David said. "It's a *representation* of a door, not the real thing."

April took a deep breath. "*I don't care.* We've done everything we know how to do; now it's time to go forward with faith. And be-sides"—she paused—"I think I'm right." She put her hands on the cold, smooth stone, braced herself, and pushed. Nothing happened. She pushed again, but this time, she noticed a tiny black-and-white spider spinning its web at the edge of the alcove. She looked over at David.

"I'm sorry," he said, "I tried to tell you—"

"Come help me," she said. "It's going to take both of us."

David shook his head. "It won't make any difference," he said, but he limped over and put his shoulder against the rock wall.

"Okay, now," April said. "We need to push as hard as we can."

Grunting with the exertion, they pressed against the back of the alcove.

With the heavy, grating sound of stone against stone, the door that wasn't a door slowly swung open.

CHAPTER 20

"I, Abraham, talked with the Lord, face to face, as one man talketh with another; and he told me of the works which his hands had made; and he said unto me: My son, my son (and his hand was stretched out), behold I will show you all these. And he put his hand upon mine eyes, and I saw those things which his hands had made, which were many; and they multiplied before mine eyes, and I could not see the end thereof. And he said unto me: This is Shinehah, which is the sun. And he said unto me: Kokob, which is star. And he said unto me: Olea, which is the moon. And he said unto me: Kokaubeam, which signifies stars, or all the great lights, which were in the firmament of heaven. And it was in the night time when the Lord spake these words unto me: I will multiply thee, and thy seed after thee, like unto these; and if thou canst count the number of sands, so shall be the number of thy seeds."—Abraham 3:11–14

The room was dark, like all the others, but the air seemed fresher, the shadows less oppressive. David looked up; the ceiling was full of stars. But this time, they weren't painted; they were real—tiny sparks of silver in a deep and endless sky. A night breeze brushed past his face. Somewhere in the distance, a dog barked, then barked again.

"I can't believe it," he said. He took a deep breath of the sweet, clean air. "We made it through. We're alive." He choked back a sob.

April took his hand. "I told you—at the end we're resurrected." Tears were streaming down her face. She laughed, wiping her eyes. "I guess we're not dead anymore."

He took her into his arms. "Thank you for coming to get me. If you hadn't found me . . ."

She smiled. "I had lots of help."

"I know." He kissed her on the forehead. "Ready to go?"

"I sure am."

David pulled out his cell phone; finally, it had a signal. Quickly, he dialed Wilcox, who picked up almost immediately.

"Hunter! Is that you? Thank goodness. Is April okay?"

"She's fine; she's right here with me."

"We were afraid you were dead."

David grimaced. "Funny you should say that."

"Why?"

"It's a long story."

"You can tell me when you get back," Wilcox said. "You know about the bomb and the earthquake, I guess."

"Yeah. How bad was it?"

"Not nearly as bad as it could have been. The bomber didn't get past the barriers, so the embassy is okay. But the guardhouse and some nearby buildings were completely destroyed."

"What about President Morales?"

"Already on her way home. You can imagine her reaction when the guardhouse was bombed. Ambassador Hodges is out on his ear."

"Wow. Are there a lot of casualties?"

"From the bomb, just a few. But they're still trying to figure out how many were killed in the quake. It did a lot of damage. Do you know where Pam is?"

"No. I haven't exactly been in a position to find out."

"Hunter, she's your *partner*. You're supposed to keep tabs on her."

"Wilcox, she's a double agent."

"You're kidding." Wilcox paused. "Are you sure?"

"She came close to ruining everything." He glanced over at April.

"Well, that does explain some things," Wilcox said. "Too bad. If it's any consolation, I guess that means you'll be the one getting the promotion."

"About that . . ."

"What?"

"I don't want it."

"Why not?"

"Field work isn't for me; it's too dangerous."

"Somebody has to do it."

"I know. But that somebody doesn't have to be me. I have a family to take care of—and we're planning to have a baby."

"Really? That's great!"

"So I was wondering if there's some position I could move into—something nice and safe. Cryptography, maybe."

Wilcox laughed. "You mean your regular job?"

"Exactly."

"I'll see what I can do. In the meantime, though, we need to get you home. The airport's shut down, at least for now."

"That's great! It means the terrorists can't get out."

"Not out of Cairo, anyway. They had no idea how much trouble they were going to cause themselves."

"I'll say."

"I suppose they could still take a boat down to Luxor and get out that way. But we'll be watching for visas approved in the days before the bombing; if we're careful, we should be able to spot them."

"I hope you're right."

"So where are you?"

"On some kind of plateau in the Muqattam Mountains, near the eastern desert. We can see the lights of the Citadel off to our left."

"Okay. I'll requisition a military helicopter. They should be there by morning to pick you up."

David looked at his watch. "That's nearly four hours away."

"Sorry I can't do better."

"We'll survive."

"You'd better. I'll expect a full report."

David closed his phone and looked at April. "They're sending a chopper. We'll be out of here by morning."

"Thank goodness. So now what do we do?"

"Wait. And rest."

"Sounds good to me. Dibs on the backpack—I mean 'pillow.'" She lay down on the sand and tucked it under her head.

"No problem," David said. "Don't mind me. I'll just use this nice rock here." He put his head down on a nearby slab of stone; it was the softest thing he'd ever felt. In just a few minutes, he was asleep.

When David woke up, the sun was starting to rise, filling the sky with glory. He looked over at April, then touched her on the shoulder.

"April, are you awake?"

She opened one eye. "I am now."

He nodded toward the sunrise. "Isn't that the most beautiful thing you've ever seen?"

April sat up, rubbing her eyes. She looked up at the clouds, which were glowing with red and gold. "Wow."

"Good morning, sunshine. Welcome to the new day."

"Same to you." She got to her feet and stretched. "How's your leg?"

He stood up, then moved his foot back and forth. "Good. I feel like a new man."

"Me too—woman, that is. At least I will after I eat one of these." She held up two granola bars.

"You've been *hoarding?*"

"I figured you'd thank me later—and by 'later,' I mean 'now.'" She handed him one of the bars.

"You really are an angel."

"I know." She picked up her backpack and took a bite of her granola bar. "What's keeping that chopper?"

"It'll be here. We should get out where they can see us better."

"Good idea."

They gathered up their things, then walked hand in hand through the two rows of enormous stone columns set up as sentinels outside the door of the temple. When they reached the end, they had to walk around a final, central column. On the other side was a magnificent statue of red granite, standing twice as tall as they were. It was a carving of the new god wearing a pharaoh's crown, with a robe over his shoulder. At his side was his wife, her hands resting on the shoulders of her son. The god's arms, in the form of wings, swept over both of them in an embrace of love and protection.

"Unbelievable," David said, touching the smooth, red stone.

"This is what the candidates would have seen at the very end of the ceremony."

"It's the family," David said. "The eternal family."

April nodded.

"It's strange," David said, "but I think I understand our own temple better now."

"Well, now you have something to compare it with. It's like English grammar—I didn't really get it until I studied French."

"Right." David sat quietly, pondering. "It's all about families. If we're faithful, eventually we can be exalted; we can create worlds and people them with children of our own."

April nodded.

"You know . . ."

"What?"

"If eventually we can do what Heavenly Father does, what does that mean about him?"

"I guess it means he used to be like us. Isn't that what the gospel teaches?"

"'As man now is, so God once was; as God now is, so man may become,'" David quoted. "I've heard it a hundred times. But this is the first time I've really *understood* it."

"God is our Father; we are his children. The new family comes into being, and the cycle of life starts again. The family of the gods continues in one great, eternal round."

"We're part of that family."

April nodded. "Let's never forget."

"We won't. Not after this."

A new thought came into David's mind. "You know the greater knowledge Abraham was seeking?"

"Yes?"

"I think I know what it is."

April smiled. "What are you thinking?"

"It's not something you know." He paused. "It's everything you *don't* know but *can* know if you keep looking deeper—everything that's *greater* than what we have now. We have to keep on growing, keep on learning, even into the eternities."

"David, that's beautiful."

"There's one more thing."

"What's that?"

"During this whole experience, *nothing* has been what it seemed—not Minkabh, not Sharifa, not Pam, not even that doorway in the tomb." He took her hand. "But you, April—out of everything we've experienced—you're the one thing that has been real and true." He took her into his arms, his voice hoarse with emotion. "I love you so much."

Then they held each other, watching the sun rise. In the distance, they heard the rhythmic chopping of helicopter wings.

EPILOGUE

"The Lord God of your fathers, the God of Abraham, of Isaac, and of Jacob, appeared unto me, saying, I have surely visited you, and seen that which is done to you in Egypt: and I have said, I will bring you up out of the affliction of Egypt . . . unto a land flowing with milk and honey."—Exodus 3:16–17

It had been more than a year since their adventure in Egypt, and David and April were enjoying their life as the parents of twins. In the corner of their new home was a Christmas tree, hung with silver stars and glowing with lights. Under it were many boxes of toys; they'd gone a little overboard.

David held Joseph on his lap. "Where's your sister?" The boy put his finger into his mouth, then looked solemnly around.

April came into the room, carrying their little girl.

"There's Rachel," David said. "She's nearly as cute as you are." He tickled the boy's stomach until the baby laughed.

David looked over at April; she was dressed for a party they were going to later, and he didn't think he'd ever seen her more beautiful. "You look great!" he said. "I love the red velvet."

"Thanks. Are these earrings okay?" She pulled at a tiny red Christmas bulb hanging from her ear.

"They're perfect."

She looked him over. "You'd better get ready; the babysitter will be here soon."

"I know. But I wanted to give you something first."

"A *present?* For *me?* Hand it over, baby."

David laughed. "Okay, okay." He pulled a small white box out of his pocket.

"I see you spent lots of time wrapping it."

"As always."

She took off the lid and brought out the tiny white stone pendant. "It's beautiful. What is it?"

"It's a heart—from Cairo. The Egyptians wore them as a reminder of what they'd have to face in the afterlife. It helped keep them out of trouble."

"And you thought I probably needed something like that."

David blushed. "Well, no. But I thought you might like it if I gave you my heart. It's yours forever, you know."

She shook her head, then looked up, tears in her eyes. "I know. I already knew."

David smiled. "It's been a great year."

"Next year will be even better."

"Is that possible?"

She nodded. "Every year from now on."

"Forever and ever, till the stars go out?"

"They won't go out." She looked at the sparkling tree. "They'll go *on,* for eternity."

"Merry Christmas," David said, looking with wonder at his beautiful wife and his beautiful children. "Merry, merry Christmas." He couldn't imagine how life could get any better. But somehow, he knew, this was just the beginning. The best was yet to come.

Notes for the Curious

Warning! Plot spoilers ahead! Don't read this until *after* you've read the novel.

This book's descriptions of Cairo and its environs are as accurate as I've been able to make them without actually having visited there. In these notes, I'll include a passage from the book, followed by commentary. Here's the first one:

Page vii: "I met a traveller from an antique land"

Percy Bysshe Shelley's famous sonnet "Ozymandias" was published in 1818. The theme is the pride of the world and its subsequent fall. *Ozymandias* was one of the names of Ramses the Great, pharaoh of Egypt's nineteenth dynasty. In fourteen short lines Shelley condensed not only the pharaoh's history but also that of an entire civilization—a powerful statement about the vanity of human ambition: *Sic transit gloria mundi.* ("Thus passes the glory of the world.")

Page 1: Abasi Mubarak thought about smoking one last cigarette before blowing himself up.

All of the Egyptian names in this book are authentic, and I've chosen them with some care. Here are the names I've used, along with their meanings:

Abasi: "Stern."

Minkabh: "Justice."

Sharifa: "Respected."

Kakra: "A twin."

Kafele: "Would die for."

Donkor: "Humble."

Baruti: "Teacher."

Runihura: "Destroyer."

Eshe: "Life."

Nekhbet: Egyptian vulture goddess.

Haqikah: "Honest."

Page 7: Much to his surprise, David found himself thinking about the contrast—the recurring growth, then death, of the fragile flowers compared to the enduring strength of the stone building. Was the temple itself a symbol of eternity?

Elder John A. Widtsoe wrote, "We live in a world of symbols. No man or woman can come out of the temple endowed as he should be, unless he has seen, beyond the symbol, the mighty realities for which the symbols stand" ("Temple Worship," *Utah Genealogical and Historical Magazine,* April 1921, 62).

Page 8: The elderly people taking part seemed so sweet and sincere, and one of the actors said his lines in such a droll way that everyone in the session chuckled from time to time.

Before the advent of film, the presentation of the endowment in LDS temples was performed by live actors. That tradition continues in two temples today: the Salt Lake Temple and the Manti Utah Temple. For more information from the Church about this:

http://www.ldschurchtemples.com/saltlake/

http://www.ldschurchtemples.com/manti/

Page 15: The shopkeeper was signaling to one of the "tourist police" stationed nearby.

The tourist police, whose job it is to protect visitors to Egypt, are a common sight in Cairo: http://img2.travelblog.org/Photos/1327/40444/t/211582-Tourist-Police-o.jpg

Page 16: The embassy building itself was huge, a blocky limestone monolith that towered over the surrounding area.

A picture is available here:

http://blog.foreignpolicy.com/node/9118

Page 16: Considering that this was an embassy of the United States of America, Pam was surprised at some of the posters the workers had taped to the walls of their cubicles—pictures with captions like "Islam: The New American Religion" and "Up with Hamas." Images of American mosques were posted everywhere.

The U.S. embassy in Cairo has had many such problems (including the unfair treatment of Christians) in recent years. For more information:

http://www.allthingsbeautiful.com/all_things_beautiful/2005/12/does_hamas_run_.html

Page 37: "You and your cigarettes. Why do you not smoke the *shisha,* like a civilized man?"

The *shisha* is a water pipe (hookah), commonly smoked in the ubiquitous Egyptian coffeehouses, often with apple-flavored tobacco.

Page 43: "This," Minkabh said as the car slowed near an ancient stone wall, "is the Necropolis—the City of the Dead."

Cairo actually has several cities of the dead, which are pretty much as I've described them in this book. And yes, human bones are readily available. For more information:

http://www.touregypt.net/featurestories/city.htm

http://www.egyptmyway.com/articles/picturescityofdead.html

Page 44: "But this is not what I brought you to see. Please, let us go on, and I will show you a much older burial complex."

The burial complex is real but in a different location, about fifteen miles south of Cairo:

http://www.msnbc.msn.com/id/5210161/

The rooms inside the complex probably have very little similarity to what I've described in this book, all of which is a product of my imagination. Nevertheless, there are numerous fascinating parallels between modern temple work and what LDS scholar Hugh Nibley called "the Egyptian endowment," as described in his monumental work *The Message of the Joseph Smith Papyri* (Salt Lake City: Deseret Book, 2005).

Page 49: "Is there any danger of the ceiling caving in?" he asked.
"If we had an earthquake, yes. In 1992 a quake in Cairo killed nearly four hundred people."

For more information on the 1992 earthquake:
http://tinyurl.com/5qg275

Pages 63–64: "'Revealing through the heavens the grand Keywords of the Priesthood,'" April read. She paused. "I'm starting to see why the temple worker said we should study the book of Abraham."

President Brigham Young taught, "Your endowment, is to receive all those ordinances in the House of the Lord, which are necessary for you, after you have departed this life, to enable you to walk back to the presence of the Father, passing the angels who stand as sentinels, being enabled to give them the key words, the signs and tokens, pertaining to the Holy Priesthood, and gain your eternal exaltation in spite of earth and hell" (in *Journal of Discourses,* 2:31).

Page 66: He pulled the computer over. "Let's see what Google says." After a little searching, they found a commentary on the book of Abraham.

I've borrowed (and slightly modified) the quoted passage from the excellent book by Richard D. Draper, S. Kent Brown, and Michael D. Rhodes, *The Pearl of Great Price: A Verse-by-Verse Commentary* (Salt Lake City: Deseret Book, 2005). This book is also my source for the Hebrew translations from the book of Abraham.

Page 97: And then David noticed: Reading the combined characters from top to bottom, they were *Kof, Lamed, Beth,* with the sounds *K, L, B,* or, as a Hebrew might say them together, *Kolob.* It was the dwelling place of God, with the very name used in the book of Abraham.

All of this is true, but I have no idea if this technique can actually be applied to other hieroglyphs, or what it really means in studying the scriptures. But it sure is interesting. For more information, see Joe Sampson, *Written by the Finger of God* (Salt Lake City: Wellspring, 1993), 149–50. FARMS has published two reviews of this book, one fairly encouraging, the other quite negative:

http://farms.byu.edu/publications/review/?reviewed_author=160

Page 122: Alone now, April got down on her knees and shined the flashlight into the hole, which was partly covered with a spiderweb. Holding the flashlight with the tips of her fingers, she used it to brush the web aside. Then she jumped as a spider, black with white markings, scurried across the edge of the hole and down into the tomb.

In ancient Egypt, the spider was associated with the goddess Neith (meaning "weaver") as the spinner and weaver of destiny. The Neoplatonic philosopher Proclus (A.D. 412–485) wrote that the temple of Neith in Sais (of which nothing now remains) bore the following inscription: "I am the things that are, that will be, and that have been" (*The Commentaries of Proclus on the Timaeus of Plato,* trans. Thomas Taylor [London: A. J. Valpy, 1820], 82).

Page 146: David groaned. "Great," he said. "We're headed back where we started."

April frowned, narrowing her eyes. "I don't think so. I think I know what this is. It's a labyrinth."

"What?"

"A labyrinth. It's like a maze. I saw one in the cathedral at Chartres."

Labyrinths are found in different configurations all over the world, including Egypt. You'll find more information here:

http://en.wikipedia.org/wiki/Labyrinth

http://www.amazeingart.com/seven-wonders/egyptian-labyrinth.html

http://www.casa.ucl.ac.uk/digital_egypt/hawara/

Page 165: "Why couldn't the characters mean exactly what they look like? The one on the right is a hand. Next are uplifted arms, meaning 'Pay attention,' 'Look,' or 'Behold.' After that comes a nail. Then there's 'Behold' again."

"So it's 'hand behold nail behold'?"

"Right. But in English we'd just say, 'Behold the hand; behold the nail.'"

I know very little about Hebrew and Egyptian, but this interpretation appears to be sound—although there seems to be some debate about whether the Paleo-Hebrew character for *hey* corresponds to modern English *H* or *E*.

http://www.walkthru.org/flash/indeedSample.swf (scroll down to page 43–44)

http://www.seekfirst.com/node/278

http://amerisoftinc.com/hebletr1.htm

http://kheph777.tripod.com/art_alephbeth/PaleoHebrew.jpg

http://yehspace.ning.com/

Page 176: "No problem," David said. "Don't mind me. I'll just use this nice rock here." He put his head down on a nearby slab of stone; it was the softest thing he'd ever felt. In just a few minutes, he was asleep.

This is an allusion to the story of Jacob as told in Genesis 28: "And Jacob went out from Beer-sheba, and went toward Haran. And he lighted upon a certain place, and tarried there all night, because the sun was set; and he took of the stones of that place, and put them for his pillows, and lay down in that place to sleep. And he dreamed, and behold a ladder set up on the earth, and the top of it reached to heaven: and behold the angels of God ascending and descending on it. And, behold, the Lord stood above it, and said, I am the Lord God of Abraham thy father, and the God of Isaac: the land whereon thou liest, to thee will I give it, and to thy seed; and thy seed shall be as the dust of the earth, and thou shalt spread abroad to the west, and to the east, and to the north, and to the south: and in thee and in thy seed shall all the families of the earth be blessed. And, behold, I am with thee, and will keep thee in all places whither thou goest, and will bring thee again into this land; for I will not leave thee, until I have done that which I have spoken to thee of. And Jacob awaked out of his sleep, and he said, Surely the Lord is in this place; and I knew it not. And he was afraid, and said, How dreadful is this place! this is none other but the house of God, and this is the gate of heaven" (Genesis 28:10–17).

Page 177: On the other side was a magnificent statue of red granite, standing twice as tall as they were. It was a carving of the new god wearing a pharaoh's crown, with a robe over his shoulder. At his side was his wife, her hands resting on the shoulders of her son. The god's arms, in the form of wings, swept over both of them in an embrace of love and protection.

For more information on family relationships, see "The Family: A Proclamation to the World":

http://www.lds.org/library/display/0,4945,161-1-11-1,00.html

Page 178: "God is our Father; we are his children. The new family comes into being, and the cycle of life starts again. The family of the gods continues in one great, eternal round."

Joseph Smith taught that the endowment is designed to give "a comprehensive view of our condition and true relation to God" (*Teachings of the Prophet Joseph Smith,* 324). The Church's priesthood and Relief Society manual for 2008 and 2009 includes the following teachings from the Prophet:

"If men do not comprehend the character of God, they do not comprehend themselves. I want to go back to the beginning, and so lift your minds into more lofty spheres and a more exalted understanding than what the human mind generally aspires to.

" . . . The scriptures inform us that 'This is life eternal, that they might know thee the only true God, and Jesus Christ, whom thou hast sent.' [John 17:3.]

"If any man does not know God, and inquires what kind of a being He is,—if he will search diligently his own heart—if the declaration of Jesus and the apostles be true, he will realize that he has not eternal life; for there can be eternal life on no other principle.

"My first object is to find out the character of the only wise and true God, and what kind of a being He is. . . .

"God Himself was once as we are now, and is an exalted man, and sits enthroned in yonder heavens! That is the great secret. If the veil were rent today, and the great God who holds this world in its orbit, and who upholds all worlds and all things by His power, was to make Himself visible,—I say, if you were to see Him today, you would see Him like a man in form—like yourselves in all the person, image, and very form as a man; for Adam was created in the very fashion, image and likeness of God, and received instruction from, and walked, talked and conversed with Him, as one man talks and communes with another. . . .

" . . . Having a knowledge of God, we begin to know how to approach Him, and how to ask so as to receive an answer. When we understand the character of God, and know how to come to Him, He begins to unfold the heavens to us, and to tell us all about it. When we are ready to come to Him, He is ready to come to us" (*Teachings of Presidents of the Church: Joseph Smith* [Salt Lake City: The Church of Jesus Christ of Latter-day Saints, 2007], 40–41).

Page 181: She took off the lid and brought out the tiny white stone pendant. "It's beautiful. What is it?"

"It's a heart—from Cairo. The Egyptians wore them as a reminder of what they'd have to face in the afterlife. It helped keep them out of trouble."

This is true enough, but I was also thinking of Revelation 2:17: "To him that overcometh will I give to eat of the hidden manna, and will give him a white stone, and in the stone a new name written, which no man knoweth saving he that receiveth it."

ACKNOWLEDGMENTS

This book could not have been published without the help of many people. In particular, I'd like to thank Colin Douglas for sharing with me his impressions of Cairo, but more especially for sharing thirty years of conversation about art, literature, politics, philosophy, history, the scriptures, the gospel, and the mysteries of eternity.

I offer my gratitude to Jana Erickson, Lisa Mangum, Emily Watts, and Jay Parry, good friends and fine editors, whose comments, questions, and suggestions have immeasurably improved this book. I'm also grateful to Anne Sheffield, Shauna Gibby, Tonya Facemyer, and Nada Midkiff at Deseret Book.

Finally, I'd like to thank my family—my mom and dad (who gave me my love of books), my wonderful wife (Anne), my spectacular kids (Rebekah, John, Matthew, and Rachel), and my terrific sisters (Suzanne, Robin, and Kathy). I also appreciate the help of my brother-in-law Wayne Williams and his wife, Karen, in refining certain elements of the plot.

About the Author

J ack Lyon, previously managing editor at Deseret Book, is a writer and publisher, the owner and operator of Waking Lion Press and Temple Hill Books. His publications include *The Moroni Code*, *Best-Loved Stories of the LDS People*, *Best-Loved Humor of the LDS People*, *The Ultimate Guide to GospeLink*, *Managing the Obvious*, *Microsoft Word for Publishing Professionals*, and several other books. At Deseret Book, he edited the *Children of the Promise* and *Hearts of the Children* novels by Dean Hughes, *The Collected Works of Hugh Nibley*, and *The Papers of Joseph Smith*, along with hundreds of other publications during a career of more than twenty-five years.

He and his wife, Anne, live in West Valley City, Utah. They have four children and six grandchildren.